NEPTUNE'S HONOR

Also by Pamela Bauer Mueller

The Kiska Trilogy

The Bumpedy Road
Rain City Cats
Eight Paws to Georgia

Hello, Goodbye, I Love You
Aloha Crossing

Historical Novels

Neptune's Honor
An Angry Drum Echoed
Splendid Isolation
Water To My Soul
Lady Unveiled

Neptune's Honor

A story of loyalty and love

Cheers!

Pamela Bauer Mueller

Pamela Bauer Mueller

PIÑATA PUBLISHING

2nd printing 2006
3rd printing 2008
4th printing 2012
5th printing 2015

Piñata Publishing
626 Old Plantation Road
Jekyll Island, GA 31527
912-635-9402

www.pinatapub.com

CANADIAN CATALOGUING IN PUBLICATION DATA

Mueller, Pamela Bauer
Neptune's honor : a story of loyalty and love / Pamela Bauer Mueller.

ISBN 13: 978-0-9685097-5-3 PBK (soft cover)
ISBN 10: 0-9685097-5-4 PBK (soft cover)

1. Small, Neptune—Fiction. 2. Slaves—Georgia—Fiction. 3. Historical fiction. I. Title.

PZ7.B324NE 2004 813'.54 C2004-904290-4

Cover art by Earnest Butts Jr.
Map on page 14 courtesy of Tommy E. Jenkins, from his book *A Graphic History of St. Simons Island*
Layout and design by the Vancouver Desktop Publishing Centre
Printed and bound in the USA by Patterson Printing

For
the descendants of Neptune Small,
with my sincere admiration.

Foreword

The story of Neptune Small is a story of courage, honor, compassion and loyalty. He was a kind and simple man who planted seeds of confidence, healing and peace throughout his seventy-five years of life. My research of pre-Civil War local plantation families, coupled with transcripts of interviews with Neptune Small, gave me a sense that he felt sincere allegiance to the family who owned him. This was not necessarily the experience of slaves living on other Georgia plantations.

An interview with Neptune Small in the Old Mill Days newspaper, entitled "Neptune's Story," was written by J.E. Dart and published in 1902. The final chapters of this book are based on Neptune's account of the Battle of Fredericksburg, and his reaction to the life-changing events that followed. I used his wording as much as possible in these chapters.

The "Black speak" dialect common during this time period was based on the Geechee-Gullah culture: a mixture of West African language with southern English. Although Neptune and some of the other slaves of this era were taught to read and write, they never completely lost their slave dialect in conversations among themselves, or with the white plantation community. Neptune's descendants have requested that his conversations be written in the dialect that appears in transcripts.

I have written this book from what I consider to be Neptune's point of view, not from a southern pro-slavery standpoint. Everyone knows that the institution of slavery was bad, and this novel is not a social commentary. It isn't possible for me to present a final and complete portrait of slavery, nor to fully comprehend this complex institution perceived differently by succeeding generations of historians.

This book is Neptune's story, yet to understand it I needed to give the reader glimpses into the lives of the King family, who "owned" him. Weddings, deaths, political and historical events, etc. are all factual, including the exact dates for these occasions.

Through extensive reading and research, I also discovered the memoirs of travelers and bondsmen from that time period. These memoirs indicate that slavery was less an "inhuman" system than an intensely "human" one in which masters and slaves lived together imperfectly, ultimately dependent on each other.

I was very fortunate to have met and interviewed Miss Creola P. Barnes, one of two remaining great-grandchildren of Neptune Small, just six weeks before she died on January 8, 2004, at the age of 83. She and her niece, Miss Diane Palmer Haywood, provided me with family memories and facts not available anywhere else. Neptune's great-great-great grandchild, Miss Angela Palmer, also shared her stories. Mr. William Barnes Jr., one of Neptune's great-great grandsons, has honored me with reading and editing the manuscript, as well as answering many questions. It has been a joy and a pleasure working with this family. My heartfelt appreciation goes out to each one of them.

"The lights of stars that were extinguished ages ago still reach us. So it is with great men who died centuries ago, but still reach us with the radiation of their personalities."

—Kahlil Gibran

DESCENDANTS OF THOMAS BUTLER KING (1797-1864) and ANNA MATILDA PAGE KING (1798-1859)

Hannah Matilda Page "Tootee" King (1825-96) m. William Audley Couper (1817-88)

- Anna Rebecca Couper (1846-1928)
- William Page Couper (1847-?)
- Isabella Hamilton Couper (1848-52)
- Butler King Couper (1851-1913)
- John Audley Couper (1853-1905)
- Helen Rosalie Couper (1855-96)
- Thomas Butler Couper (1858-1909)

William Page King (1826-33)

Thomas Butler "Buttie" King (1829-59)

Henry Lord Page "Lordy" King (1831-62)

Georgia Page King (1833-1914) m. Wiliam Duncan Smith (1826-62)
m. Joseph John Wilder (1844-1900)

- Anne Page Wilder (1873-1956)

Florence Barclay "Flo" King (1834-1912) m. Henry Rootes Jackson (1820-98)

Mallery Page "Malley" King (1836-99) m. Maria Eugenia Grant (1836-1909)

- Mary Anna Page King (1867-1946)
- Frances Buford King (1869-1956)
- Florence Page King (1871-1955)
- Thomas Butler King (1875-77)

Virginia Lord "Appy" King (1837-1901) m. John Nisbet (1841-1917)
- John Lord Nisbet (1872-1938)
- Marianne Nisbet (1874-1947)
- Florence King Nisbet (1877-1963)
- Virginia Lord Nisbet (1879-1963)
- Nannie Page Nisbet (1880-1927)

John Floyd "Fuddy" King (1839-1915)

Richard Cuyler "Tip" King (1840-1913) m. Henrietta Dawson Nisbet (1863-1944)
- Henry Lord Page King (1895-1952)
- Mary Nisbet King (1900-1970)

Information courtesy of Edwin R. MacKethan III *and Melanie Pavich-Lindsay*

DESCENDANTS OF NEPTUNE Sr. (b. August 4, 1796) AND SUKEY (? 1800-June 1, 1852)

From Anna Matilda King's Estate Inventory and other sources

Abner (b. October 1, 1820)

Liddy (b. April 15, 1823) **m. Alfred** (b. December 3, 1822)
  Frederick (b. February 3, 1843)
  Adilette (b. September 26, 1847)
  Liddy (?)
  Peter (b. October 1863)

Sanders (b. September 4, 1827)

Neptune (September 15, 1831-August 10, 1907)
 m. Ila (December 30, 1834)
  Leanora (b. October 1859)
  Louturia (?)
  Clementine (?)
  Cornielia (?)
  Clarence (?)

Emiline (August 3, 1833-May 1852)

Mily (? 1836-May 1852)

Linda (b. April 29, 1838) **m. James (Jimper)** (b. January 25, 1829)
  Jim (b. December 1861)
  Casina (b. April 1864)
  Rosey (?)
  Christian (?)

Walter (?)

Information courtesy of William Barnes Jr., Edwin R. MacKethan III, and Melanie Pavich-Lindsay

Prologue

December 1862

"Yo' family be so happy wen you git home, Mas' Lordy. But first, we gunna rest in Richmon', an' git you a nicer box. I want you be lookin' fine b'for we gits to Savannah."

Captain Henry Lord King didn't answer him.

"Soon you be restin' good back at S'n Simons Islan', but we cain't go dere now. Dem Nordern Yankees still livin' in Retreat Plantation, an' de officers telling me it not safe to take you dere." Bell snorted and her breath fogged the frigid air when Neptune reached over to rub her nose. Her hooves crunched through packed snow as she transported her precious cargo through the dense forest, still filled with smoke and pain.

Despite the bitter cold, Neptune began feeling a sense of peace and warmth flow through him. He winced as he gradually came to realize that life chooses its consequential moments without consulting those who are living them.

For the next hour or so, Neptune spoke tenderly to Lordy about their childhood. His heart swelled with pleasure as he remembered the fishing trips, turtle egg hunts, horseback rides, and island hunting. Yet even when reliving so many enjoyable times, his heart was shrouded in sorrow. He kept talking, knowing the pain of speaking from his heart was more tolerable than the endless suffering of silence.

He urged Bell to pick up the pace so they could get Lordy back home. Reaching an opening in the sunlit cathedral of snow-fringed pines, he heard the oddest sound: like a fluttering of heavy wings.

The clear winter morning melted into stillness. Neptune glanced over his shoulder at Master Lordy and smiled wistfully in understanding. It was the sound of a soul flying away.

Contents

Childhood / 15

Boyhood / 43

Adulthood / 107

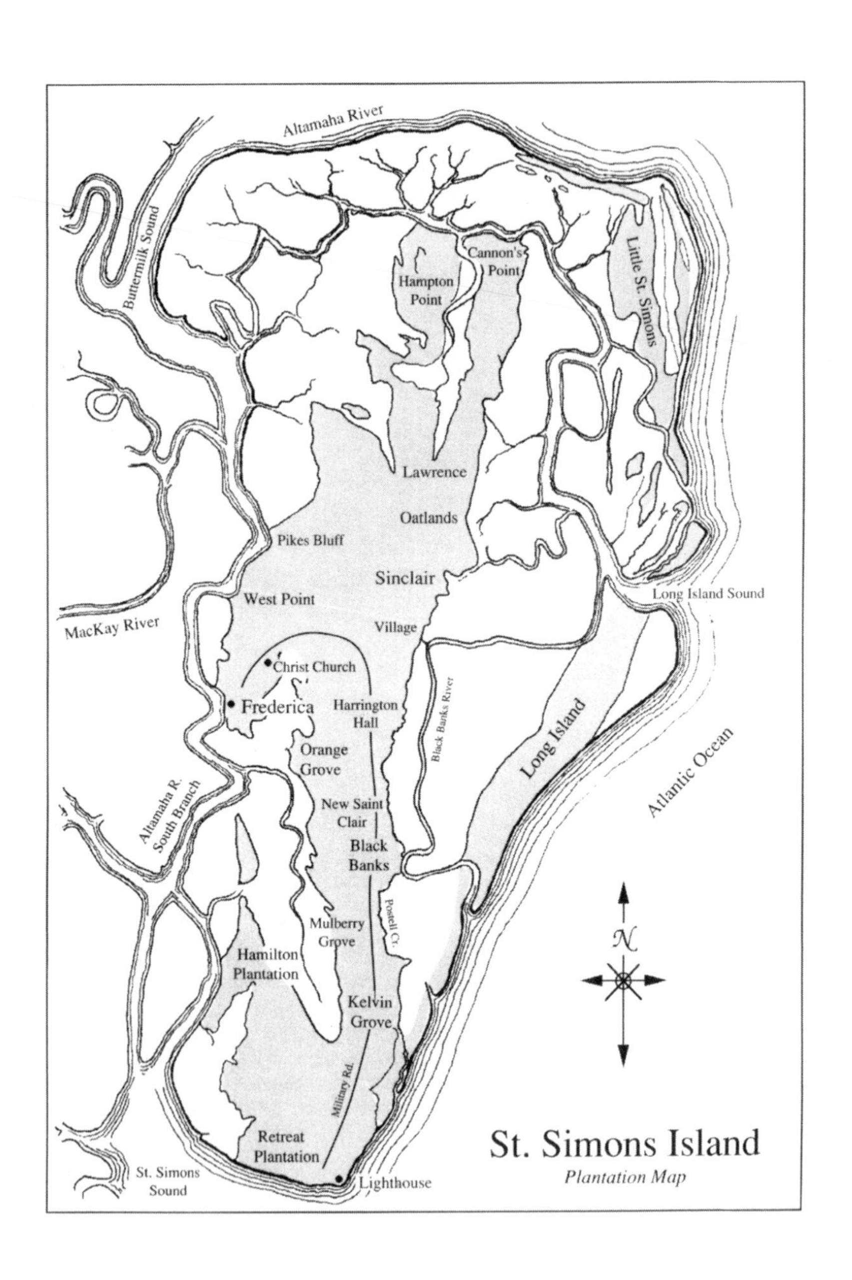
Altamaha River
Buttermilk Sound
Little St. Simons
Cannon's Point
Hampton Point
Lawrence
Oatlands
Pikes Bluff
Sinclair
West Point
Long Island Sound
MacKay River
Village
Christ Church
Frederica
Harrington Hall
Black Banks River
Long Island
Orange Grove
Atlantic Ocean
Altamaha R. South Branch
New Saint Clair
Black Banks
Postell Cr.
Mulberry Grove
N
Hamilton Plantation
Kelvin Grove
Military Rd.
Retreat Plantation
St. Simons Sound
Lighthouse
St. Simons Island
Plantation Map

Childhood

Chapter One

August 5, 1837

Howling winds awoke Neptune with a start. He bolted upright on his mat and reached in the darkness toward Lordy's bed. It was warm, but empty. As his eyes slowly adjusted, Neptune could see Lordy standing across the room next to the high front window. A savage clap of thunder boomed through the bedroom and sent Neptune scurrying over the cool wooden floorboards. The banging shutters made him jump as he groped in the darkness to find his friend.

"Wat's happnin', Mas' Lordy? I sho' be skired wif dat noise," he whimpered as he grabbed onto his hand.

"Me too, Neptune. Let's go find my Mama."

They were still stumbling through the darkness when Lordy's mother, Anna Matilda King, appeared at the doorway with Tootee and Buttie at her heels, holding on tightly to Georgia's tiny hand. Anna's loyal servant Maum Lady was right behind them, lighting their way with a large candlestick. She carried toddler Malley over her wide hip, while little Flo grabbed at her long robe, eyes wide with fright.

"Mama, is this a hurricane?" whispered Tootee, sounding surprisingly grown-up for a twelve-year old.

Anna Matilda hesitated. "I don't know, sweetie, but I'm counting on you to help me with the little ones." Her uncertain smile only partially concealed her fear.

Anna Matilda ushered them all downstairs to the parlor,

soothing them with her calming words and silently praying for guidance. Being heavy with child considerably slowed down her movements. Her older sons and Maum Lady set up pillows and cushions for the others on the floor as she quietly stood by and smiled in gratitude. Finally, she arranged herself in a large chair near the door and held fussy little Flo in her arms. The boys sat at her feet, offering her some comfort in the absence of their father, Thomas Butler King.

Through the windows Neptune saw the heavy branches of the live oaks and magnolias whipping wildly, then snapping and flying across the yard. The field fence was blown flat to the ground. The winds screamed through the walls of their home, and Neptune could only imagine the damage to their beautiful garden. One window was blown loose and the children squealed as the glass smashed and rain pelted through the opening.

Neptune watched and listened, sitting stiffly next to Lordy but wishing he could run down the porch and across the field to his own family, who lived in a slave cabin behind the summer kitchen. He would have been there with them, except last night Lordy asked him to sleep over in the big house. Neptune squeezed his eyes tightly and tried to think happy thoughts, just as his mother Sukey had taught him to do.

He heard Anna Matilda pray for their safety and for her husband Thomas. She was relieved that he was in the capital city of Milledgeville, far away from the coastal storms. She thanked God that they were now living on Georgia's mainland in one of their smaller plantations, rather than at Retreat Plantation on St. Simons Island. She feared the winds would be roaring even more savagely there during the brunt of the storm.

"Dear Heavenly Father, please be with all my people who are still living at Retreat, and keep them safe from harm. Watch over my children and our servants accompanying us here at

Monticello, and give my beloved Thomas peace and travel mercies when he returns to us." Neptune knew Anna Matilda always felt better after sharing her fears with God.

Time passed slowly as the children slept and Anna Matilda sat in her parlor, waiting for daylight to appear. Maum Lady kept vigil with her mistress, squeezing her hand for comfort and humming softly in an attempt to drown out the shrieking gale.

Neptune knew his parents were safe in their cabin, but his mind was filled with images of the wind. Finally, in spite of the crashing noises of the flowerpots and outdoor furniture tossed in every direction, he fell into an exhausted sleep.

At the first light of sunrise, Neptune awoke to see the skies open up and the rain begin to fall. It started slowly and lazily, and then formed heavy noisy sheets, competing with the shrill wind. Smiling at God's sense of humor in granting her the long awaited water for the crops and flowers, Anna Matilda sighed deeply and fell asleep.

Chapter Two

August 6, 1837

The storm raged throughout Sunday, battering the Georgia coastline and keeping everyone behind bolted doors. The other servants could not leave their quarters to help out in the main house, so Maum Lady and the Scottish nanny, Mammy Gale, did as much for Anna Matilda and the children as they could. There was little to eat, since they stored most of the food in the summer kitchen outside.

The heavens stormed from morning to darkness. Neptune and the children grew restless, pacing like prisoners. The older ones tried to read to their younger siblings, but soon everyone lost interest in the books. Neptune followed Lordy closely, trying to anticipate his needs.

"Neptune, let's play that game your Mama showed us with the marbles," Lordy suggested in the early afternoon.

"Mas' Lordy, you sho' kin play nice wen you a winnin' but you owes me two cat-eyes dat I ain't got jet." Neptune smiled slyly, nudging his friend.

"I wanna play too," interrupted little Georgia, as always wanting to be with her brother and Neptune. "I got three cat's-eye marbles."

Lordy and Neptune were born five months apart. Lordy was born on April 25, 1831 and Neptune followed him into the world on September 15. Although Neptune was born into slavery and Henry Lord Page King was the son of the plantation owner, the boys loved each other as brothers. With his sweet disposition and intelligence, Neptune had been chosen to be a playmate for the three older boys, William Page, Thomas Butler Jr. and Henry Lord Page. Neptune and Lordy quickly became very compatible, and at six they were already beginning to share toys and secrets.

Soon all the children, including Rhina's daughter Peggy, the slave playmate for the King girls, were arguing and laughing while they played with their marbles and cards. Anna Matilda watched them, a smile slowly lighting up her face as she counted her blessings. Her husband would soon return from the State Senate and she would present him with another child! All of her six living children were well and happy.

The storm jogged Anna's memory back to a much sadder day, when she lost her oldest son, William Page King, at the age of six. He had been the same age that Lordy and Neptune were now. Hour after hour she sat by his sick bed, watching helplessly as he was consumed by the fever caused by an infection. For two days and nights she held his little hand and prayed, only to have to let him go in the end. Loyal Maum Lady and her daughter Sally had kept watch with her, so their mistress wouldn't have to keep this sorrowful vigil alone. Once again, her husband had been away, campaigning for the Georgia State Senate position that he still held.

Anna Matilda shuddered, recalling that time as the worst period of her life. After William died in their plantation home on St. Simons Island, she felt she could never return there to live. This mainland house in Wayne County had just been built, and it was here that she brought her entire family. At least in this house, Monticello, she didn't see sweet William's face in every room or hear his happy chatter as he raced around the grounds.

During her lonely times, like today, she yearned to be on the island with her childhood friends. How she missed them and needed them, especially dear Anne Fraser. She found herself daydreaming about those glorious pink and red sunsets filled with mystery. She missed living next to the sea! Would she return one day to her St. Simons home?

She was happy here in Monticello, a tall-columned Greek Revival mansion. They often visited and entertained at their other plantation, Waverly, in nearby Camden County, where Thomas grew rice in fields that stretched eight miles along the Satilla River. While she loved both of mainland houses, she was slowly realizing that she pined for that home on the sea where three of her children were born.

Hannah Page (Tootee) and Thomas Butler Jr. (Buttie) were born during two different visits to Brooklyn, New York. Florence Barclay (Flo) and Mallery Page (Malley) were delivered here on the mainland, and William Page, Henry Lord Page (Lordy) and Georgia were born in their large bedroom back home at Retreat Plantation. Soon the new baby would arrive here at Monticello. Thomas had promised to be home for the birth, and Anna Matilda fervently hoped that he could keep that promise.

The long day passed slowly. Then on Monday morning, a rattling of buckets on the front porch awoke Neptune. The rest of the slaves, dripping wet and whistling, somehow made their way through the heavy winds to the main house. Neptune rushed to the door to greet them, knowing his family would be among them. Missus Anna Matilda joined him and unbolted the door to welcome them. Their hands were filled with eggs from the disoriented remaining chickens and ham cured and dried from earlier times.

Taking quick inventory of her rain soaked and smiling slaves, Anna Matilda joined them in the breakfast preparations for her noisy crowd. Neptune rushed to his mother, Sukey, to dry off her rain-drenched head.

"Rhina, do you think it's over?" Anna Matilda asked one of her cooks, who was busily stirring a pot of cheese grits over the fire.

"It be mos' finish, Missus. Dem trees be blowin' quieter now. Tank de Lord, Missus, we's here an' soon our Mausa be here too!" Rhina, who always spoke cheerfully and optimistically, was spreading much needed happiness into the parlor that morning.

From the doorway, Anna Matilda turned to give Rhina and Sukey a warm reassuring smile. Neptune, noticing the gesture, was reminded of a conversation he overheard in his cabin a few days ago between his parents. Sukey had told his father how fortunate they were to live in their clean bright cabin, while some "free people of color" didn't have such good conditions. Neptune wanted to ask Lordy about that, or maybe even his parents.

"Come an' git dese biskits wile dey be so hot dey make de buttah swim!" laughed Sukey, standing in the pantry and beckoning them with her huge smile.

After a hearty breakfast, the children returned to their games with renewed energy. Tootee took out her sewing kit and joined her mother in the parlor.

"Mama, there's something weighing heavy on my mind. I've noticed that all of us living here in coastal Georgia call our slaves 'our people' or 'our servants.' Yet when we receive letters from Savannah or further up north, our friends refer to them as slaves. Why is this?"

"Hmm, as long as I can remember, my parents and their friends called them 'their people.' It sounds wrong to call our people 'slaves,' even though legally we do own them," replied Anna Matilda. "Here in the low country we care about them deeply; since they really are part of our family."

As she paused a slow smile crossed her face. "Do not forget that we islanders are very good to our people, as they are to us. At least most of us are kind, although there is one plantation owner who treats his slaves like cattle." Anna Matilda shook her head sadly, thinking about the one family that definitely treated their servants with disrespect and even cruelty.

Tootee looked up from her work to regard her mother.

"Mama, are you comfortable or uncomfortable owning slaves?" she asked pointedly.

Anna Matilda set down her needlepoint and walked over to her daughter, looking down at her inquisitive face.

"Well, dear, I think I'm a little of both," she answered in her tender voice. "I grew up with this custom. Planters on St. Simons Island owned people. In order to work our plantations, we had no choice."

Neptune, listening from the next room, was absorbing every word.

"Does calling them people instead of slaves make you feel more at ease about it?" Tootee was clearly struggling with her own feelings.

"Perhaps. I feel that it dignifies them as well." Anna Matilda had recently written a letter about this to a friend in Savannah. It had been difficult to put her feelings in writing.

Neptune scooted closer to the door, trying to make some sense out of this very grown-up conversation. Tonight during supper at his house he would talk this over with his parents.

That evening Neptune spoke up.

"Papa, why do de white people talk 'bout us b'longin' to dem? An' den always axin' each oder if we be happy?" he asked.

Neptune's older brothers, Abner and Sanders, looked at him curiously, wondering what he had heard and from whom. His father paused a few moments, and then answered him.

"Son, we do b'long to de King family. Dey be good to us an' we hab de bes' life dey kin give us. But dis life be forced on us. Nobody kin be truly happy if you ain't free."

Neptune's father continued, his eyes on his son. "You see, I's a good carpentah but cain't git paid fer my work cuz I be a slave. If I was a free man, I make money an' take care ob dis family, like oder free men does. Das wat I dream of!" he spoke urgently, dark eyes shining.

Saddened by her husband's inability to realize his dreams, Sukey gently took his hand and turned to Neptune.

"Yo' Papa be right, Neptune. He kin only be de man in control here in our cabin. On de plantation, he jes be a slave an dat's it. All peoples wanna control dere family's lives, but we cain't. We hab' no say ober wats happin' to our chillins. If de King family has to sell us an' split us up, dere ain't nuthin' yo' Papa an' me could do bout dat. Kin you understand wat we telling you?"

"Yes, Mama. We not be free but we hab' a good family wif de Kings," answered Neptune. His face broke into a smile.

"An' Papa, I be de mos' lucky boy cuz you be my Papa." Neptune's eyes were gleaming with pride as he climbed on his father's lap and gave him a kiss.

The rains slowly abated over the next three days, leaving drenched fields and bare, bowed trees. As soon as it was safe to go from the island to the mainland, several of their servants rowed over from Retreat Plantation to bring them the sad news of Dr. Fraser's death. William Fraser was the husband of one of Anna Matilda's dearest childhood friends, Frances Whylly Fraser, and Anna knew they all must go to her as quickly as they could.

On the afternoon of the third day, with gray and still menacing skies but no more rainfall, Neptune joined the King family and other servants on their schooner for the sail to St. Simons Island. From the storm-wracked wharf at Frederica, they got their first glimpse of the destruction that lay across the shores and fields of their island. Yet tiny pale green moss and lichen flowers were popping out everywhere, adding an air of enchantment to the island.

"What do you suppose happened to our home, our precious Retreat Plantation?" Anna Matilda whispered to Tootee as they stepped from the boat. Before Tootee could compose her thoughts to answer her mother, Anna Matilda felt a strong sense that one day she would return to live on her island.

Chapter Three

August 15, 1837

At Retreat Plantation or at Monticello, Thomas King's children started lessons at age five; first with Mammy Gale, their Scottish nanny, and later with their mother and private tutors. Their black foster siblings were encouraged to study with them. This was a rather unusual practice on a few of the plantations in coastal Georgia; some other plantation owners were critical of the Kings and those who taught the slaves to read. Still, Anna Matilda King insisted that her children's slave playmates receive lessons along with her own. This was done in defiance of the rumor that it was against Georgia law for slaves to be educated.

The children of both races enjoyed this fellowship, and it enabled some of the slave children to teach their parents and friends to read as well.

Neptune spent most of the day with the King children, but slept in the slave cabin with his family at night. His mother Sukey explained to him that he had been selected to be a foster brother or playmate for the older boys, just as Rhina's daughter Peggy was chosen as Tootee's playmate. Sukey said that when Peggy and Neptune grew older they would be trained to be a lady's maid and a body servant, and would accompany the King children throughout their lifetimes. They could marry and have families, but would live wherever their white "siblings" lived. Neptune thought that would be fun.

Neptune and Peggy understood that even though they played

with their white friends, they were also expected to spend time with their black companions. Their parents wanted them to learn their African customs and language and took great pride in teaching them their traditions.

Since Neptune's mother Sukey worked in the kitchen with Maum Lady and several other women, their family lived in a small cabin close to the big house. All of the servants' quarters were built out of tabby, which was a mixture of sand, water, lime and oyster shells. The cabins were built for two families, divided by a closed wall. The first floor contained two rooms. There was a dormitory second floor, a set of stairs and a fireplace that opened on both sides of the house from a central chimney. Often the parents slept in one room, the male children in another, and the girls in the third. If the family was small, the third room was used as an eating and socializing room; otherwise, the small space in between the bedrooms was closed off for eating.

On Retreat Plantation, most of the field hands lived one mile away from the main house in slave cabins near the cotton fields, in the area known as New Field. When they visited Retreat, Neptune and the King boys liked to go over to New Field to play with their slave children friends.

Slave children were not expected to work until they were about twelve years old. At age ten or eleven they were allowed to apprentice under the craftsmen if they wanted to learn how to shoe the horses or work with wood or metal. The slaves were the best cabinetmakers on the island and had learned the trade at a very young age from both black and white craftsmen. The children usually played in the fields behind where their parents worked. The younger ones stayed at the slave quarters and were cared for by the older slaves who no longer worked the fields.

All the children on the plantation shared daytime activities, especially during their first eight years. One thing they loved to do was build wagons and carts to race down the slopes and small hills they cleared out in the forest. Often while they played, they sang "ring-play" songs, like "*Emma, You My Darlin'*." Then they would dance on their knees to the beat of a tin kettle, accompanied by animated hand clapping. Black and white children competed fiercely for the honor of being the best singer and dancer. After they grew up, the plantation children in coastal Georgia passed these songs on to their children.

Neptune may have been only six years old, but already he understood that he had a special place in the King household. When he was away from Lordy, Sukey and Neptune made certain that he was not treated any differently than his brothers, Abner and Sanders, or his sister Liddy. They understood that although Neptune had the run of the King plantation, as a slave he would never be one of them and would need a close family of his own.

Sometimes Neptune and Lordy were having such a good time together that Lordy would ask him to stay and sleep in his room. This usually happened during those long warm summer evenings when the skies were still light right up to their bedtime. During these times, Neptune slept on a mat beside Lordy's bed.

Neptune and Lordy acted like twins. Being so close in age and spending all their time together, they could almost read each other's mind. While Lordy was a tall boy with long thin limbs, Neptune was short and wiry. Both boys had black curly hair and dark eyes. Neptune's eyes were chestnut brown while Lordy's were the shade of light honey. The boys even had similar mischievous personalities.

Lordy interrupted lessons this morning by asking Mammy Gale about the ghost of Mulberry Grove.

"Why Lordy, I don't know a thing about any ghost in Mulberry Grove Plantation. Why do you ask?" Mammy Gale was from Scotland and very proper in her manners.

"Because my older brother and sister told me she exists. Neptune and I want to know her story," answered Lordy with determination.

Neptune raised his eyebrows. He had no idea that Lordy would include him in this impertinence. Turning to Lordy, he whispered for him to stop being rude.

"You will both pay attention to class this moment or I will speak to Miss Anna Matilda about your manners," scolded Mammy Gale, sweeping her wide forehead with the back of her hand in a rather dramatic gesture. Buttie and Georgia stifled their giggles, while Tootee frowned her disapproval.

At dinner that evening, Lordy asked Anna Matilda to tell them about the ghost. Smiling with amusement, she began her tale.

"Some years back," she began, "during the year of the hurricane, 1824, and before any of you were born, there lived a lovely young lady named Mary. She was the ward of old Raymond Demere of Mulberry Grove, the plantation right down the lane from Retreat. Anyway, Mary fell in love with old Raymond's son and he with her. Just before the hurricane broke loose, he went to the mainland for some business and promised Mary he would return that same day. All afternoon and into the night Mary waited for him, watching as the waves thundered on the shore and listening to the wind roaring in from the sea.

"When it grew dark, she took a lantern and went to the highest part of the house to keep her vigil. From there she could see his capsized boat half-submerged beneath the savage waves. Sobbing with grief, she realized that he had drowned trying to keep his promise to return to her. Without a word to anyone, she ran into the water and drowned herself to join him in the stormy sea." Anna Matilda hesitated, noticing the disturbed expressions on their faces.

"Mama, why would she want to die?" asked Buttie in disbelief.

"Because, dear heart, sometimes love can be so strong between two people that if one is gone, the other one doesn't want to be left behind. Maybe she thought they would meet again in Heaven."

"What happened next?" asked Tootee.

"Well, they say the ghost of Mary the Wanderer haunts the path she followed when she ran down to the water. Some say you can hear her crying if you walk that path at night. But of course that's just a story, and I don't believe she's a ghost. I think she went on to her eternal life and joined her love." Anna Matilda ended thoughtfully.

Neptune's eyes were wide with interest. He had heard about "Mary de Wander" from his family. They said they could hear her sobbing late at night when they walked down that path. He glanced over at Lordy, who seemed to be thinking the same thing.

After dinner the night of the ghost story, Lordy grabbed Neptune's arm and pulled him away from the others.

"I want to go find Mary's ghost. Will you come with me?" he asked excitedly.

"How we gunna do dat, Mas' Lordy? We jes kids. We gotta go wif sum adults, an' who gunna wanna take us?"

Lordy hesitated, and then looked exasperated. "You talk to your uncles and see who will take us. Or maybe Tootee will go. We have to do this before we go back to Monticello!" He was thinking quickly, grasping for solutions.

"Okay, Mas' Lordy, I sees wat I kin do. It be good to find de ghost," agreed Neptune.

The boys could find no one to take them to find Mary's ghost during that visit. But eventually they did walk Mary the Wanderer's haunted path. Two years later they found the opportunity.

One summer at twilight, Neptune's father agreed to take them all down Mary's path. Tootee, Buttie, Lordy, Neptune and Thomas Butler King went along, encouraged by the young boys' enthusiasm. All were deeply disappointed when they neither saw nor heard her ghost.

Lordy and Neptune returned a few years later as teenagers, and once again left discouraged. They never admitted to hearing Mary's cries or feeling her presence.

Chapter Four

August 30, 1837

Tootee sat under the grand oak tree and wrote in her diary, keeping an eye on Lordy and Neptune. The boys scurried up the tree in their excitement to swing over the creek on the thick, twisted bullis grape vines, and then land with a splash in the water. Both of them loved the anticipation of hanging on the vine suspended over the creek, and then plunging into the water. The ever-present chickens seemed to wait, squawking and scurrying each time the boys let loose of the vines too early, missing the water and landing in their midst with a thump and a yelp. Howling with laughter, they'd scramble up the tree again to start all over. Eventually, they tired of the game.

"Hey, Tootee, let me choose the watermelon," declared Lordy, returning hungry and standing over a row of melons in the nearby cart. This was the most fun part of the picnic Tootee had prepared for them.

To find the ripest watermelon, they placed a stem of Bahia grass over the width of the melon. If it slowly turned and ended up lying over the length of the fruit, that meant it was ready to eat.

"Mas' Lordy, it not be yo' turn. Today it be Mas' Buttie's turn," protested Neptune. "An' since he not here, I gunna choose de melon, cuz you choose de las' time." Neptune carefully set the stems of Bahia grass on top of each one and found the ripest one of the bunch.

Soon they had filled their tummies and sat back, drowsy and relaxed. Each one stretched out on the grass and watched Tootee walk back to the house. The boys were seldom left unsupervised.

Lying under the shaded oaks and watching a pileated woodpecker chipping off whole shingles from the nearby pine, they felt a sense of peace. Far across the meadow they could see the rice fields, where field hands' voices were raised in song, imploring the winds to blow the husks from the grain.

"*New rice an' okra—Nana-Nana!*
Eat some an' leave some—Nana-Nana!
Beat rice to bum-bum
Eat some an' leave some—Nana-Nana!"

Neptune rolled over on his side and asked Lordy if he wanted to go down to the creek.

"Uh huh, I do. Let's go skip rocks and swim," replied Lordy with a mischievous grin.

"Mas' Lordy, you crazier den a Betsy bug! You know we cain't swim wifout de grown-ups. We jes go dere and set and skip dem stones." Neptune scolded him with a wagging finger.

"Okay, stop fussing at me. You sound just like Tootee."

They walked toward the gurgling water and listened to the sweet birdcalls in the trees above. The musty earth odors of the marsh reached their nostrils and settled as they continued forward. Suddenly a *swoosh* sound startled them from overhead. A magnificent osprey was diving into the golden marsh grasses directly in front of them, searching for food.

"Hey, that was close!" exclaimed Lordy in awe. "Now if we see a blue heron too Buttie will have to give me all his best marbles!"

Settling down on flat rocks next to the creek, they tossed some small stones and challenged each other to see whose pebbles skipped faster and further. Neptune finally conceded that Lordy had won.

Sweating and itching from the heat, they agreed to wade halfway into the water to cool off from the relentless sun.

"Ahh, oh yes, this feels good, doesn't it?" said Lordy.

Suddenly there was a splash and a harsh release of air coming from Lordy's mouth. Neptune's eyes widened as he watched his friend tumble face first into the water, bracing his fall with his hands. Neptune scrambled over the rocks to grab Lordy's arm and pull him back to safety at the water's edge.

"Oww, oh, be careful. My foot hurts!" Lordy cried out in pain, tears quickly filling his eyes.

"Watsa matta, Mas' Lordy? Wat happen to yo' foot?"

Lordy hesitated, as if he wanted to say something like "nothing, it's okay," but instead answered very seriously. "I think I twisted it on a rock when I fell."

They sat down and looked at his ankle. Red from the cold water, it looked like it was beginning to swell up. Lordy cringed and cried out when they touched it.

"Neptune, how are we gonna walk home? It's too far!" he asked with dismay and frustration.

"You jes set yoself here an' I gunna run to dem rice fields an' get us sum help. I be rat back, Mas' Lordy."

Neptune took off at full speed, his strong thin legs pumping and his heart racing wildly. He quickly reached the rice fields and collapsed, trying to explain the predicament to the field hands and gasping for breath as the words tumbled out. Muscular Lucas pulled him up and volunteered to return with him to the creek. Even running slowly, Neptune could barely keep up with Lucas's long strides.

When they reached the creek, they found Lordy cooling his ankle in the frigid water. Lucas smiled broadly and gently lifted him onto his expansive shoulders to carry him back to the Monticello house.

"Be still now, Mas' Lordy. You set rat dere for a spell." Lucas set him down gently on the porch rocker and went in search of Maum Lady to bring ice.

Lordy studied Neptune for a minute.

"You know, if you didn't run for help I'd still be back at the stream with my foot swelling up." He winced from pain as he looked at Neptune. "Will you always help me get home?"

Neptune felt strange and wasn't sure that he understood the question. But he took Lordy's hand and spoke from his heart.

"Always," he answered honestly.

Maum Lady came bursting through the screen door, carrying a white enamel bowl filled with ice.

"Oh, Honey Chile, whatsa happnin' to yo' foot? Y'all let Maum Lady fix it up," she cooed to him as the tears dribbled down his cheeks. "Neptune, go fetch yo' mama rat now." Sukey always seemed to know exactly what to do in any situation.

That evening the family took turns indulging Lordy in his every whim. No one seemed concerned that he and Neptune had disobeyed his father's orders and gone into the water by themselves. The sprained ankle was the topic of conversation and Neptune was considered a hero, along with Lucas, Maum Lady and Sukey. Several hours later, two very tired little boys closed their eyes and fell into deep undisturbed sleep.

Chapter Five

September 14, 1839

The large wooden plantation boat eased into the dock at Retreat Plantation. Neptune and the King children raced up the shore to the house. Anna Matilda had not joined them on this trip, but sent the children's tutor, Mammy Gale, and her head oarsman Quamina along with the six rowers. Soon her best friend Anne Fraser's children would be arriving, and their other good friends, the Goulds, were coming for evening turtle egg hunting down on the beach.

Finding turtle eggs was one of their favorite adventures. Lordy imagined he was alone on a desert island, depending on his wits to survive and then finding this great delicacy. The turtle egg hunts appealed to Neptune's reverent feelings about the wondrous beauty of nature. He wondered: if a clumsy, ugly beast such as a loggerhead turtle could produce something as delicate and hopeful as a turtle egg, what might he become if he set his mind to it?

The older children, Tootee and Buttie, ran ahead and raced each other up the path. They were so excited to be back home; they had lived at Retreat longer than any other house. When their dignified plantation house came into view, with its tree-lined roads, shuttered porches and glorious gardens, they let out a holler of delight. As they ran up the cedar and cypress lined roads to the gardens, the sea breezes lifted up the fragrance of their roses. Everyone agreed that Mama's roses had a perfume sweeter than any others on the island. The tall roofs of the plantation house were framed with stately oak trees and draped in veils of Spanish moss, forming canopies of greens, browns and grays.

"Maum Lady, we're back! Where are you?" shouted Buttie as he ran through the foyer. Maum Lady had always been in charge of the plantation house. In preparation for the children's visit, Anna Matilda had sent her back to the island last week.

"Lord hab mercy! Here you be!" She rushed out to wrap them in her strong brown arms, her copper eyes shining with glee. "Were's Lordy, Georgia an' Lil' Neptune?"

"Here we are! We got shorter legs so they always beat us," squealed Georgia, pushing Tootee aside to find room in Maum Lady's warm embrace.

"Well, I jes fixin' to heat up a big dinnah of corn beef, fried catfish, collard greens an' black-eyed peas, so come on in an' set yo'selfs down." Maum Lady was overjoyed to see the children again and watch over them for her Missus.

"Hullo, Maum Lady. I sho' did miss you wen you left us at Monticello," smiled Neptune, slipping quietly behind her to hug her ample frame.

"Honey Chile, you be missed too! I bake yo' favorite biskits. Come on now to de table."

They ate hungrily and enjoyed food so delicious it made them smack their lips in appreciation. When they could eat no more they talked loudly and happily, drowning out each other's suggested plans for the rest of the day.

Finally they agreed to first go shrimping with Quamina and Jules. Then, when the low tide moved in, they would go to the mudflats for oysters and clams. After supper everyone would walk down to the beach with their good friend Mary Gould, who had promised to show them where the loggerhead turtles hid their eggs.

They followed Quamina and Jules through the cotton fields to the creek bank.

"Listen!" exclaimed Tootee with a grin. Remember this song?" She jerked her thumb toward the other end of the field and the rhythmic, yodel sounding melodies coming from the cotton fields just beyond the trees.

The children ran to the edge of the forest and waved wildly to the slaves, who returned their greetings with shouts of welcome. The fishing party joined in the singing as they headed down toward the creek.

"Pay me, Oh Pay Me
Pay me my money down.
Pay me or go to jail
Pay me my money down.
Think I heard my captain say
Pay me my money down.
T'morrow is my sailing day
Pay me my money down.
Wish't I was Mas' King's son
Pay me my money down
Stay in the house and drink good rum
Pay me my money down."

When the work was heavy and concerted effort was required, the slaves sang to each other across the fields. One man sang the first line, and the others would answer in response singing, always at a moderate tempo. The sweetness of tone carried across the cotton plants and into the clear sunny forest. This was a special song because the workers personalized their sentiments by adding the King family's name to the lyrics.

Slave men and slave women planted, hoed and harvested the

cotton. The men usually wielded the heavy hoes, but on Retreat Plantation they also had the use of two plows. The light sandy soil contained few stones, so hoeing was efficient and cost effective.

The King children and their friends reached the mudflats at low tide. Jules and Quamina unfolded and checked their seine fishing nets for holes before shrimping. Neptune and Lordy pulled the nets along the creek bottoms, enjoying the sport of tossing them so they opened up to allow the shrimp in, before sinking back to the bottom. Tootee and her brothers scrambled down the creek banks to search for oysters and clams.

"This is so easy today! I like shrimping here on the island much better than over at Monticello, don't you, Neptune?" Lordy shouted across the water.

Neptune nodded and shouted back. "I like it bof places, Mas' Lordy. I like to be wif y'all were evah you be fishin'," he answered good-naturedly.

Georgia joined them after a while, singing in her clear soprano voice and tossing the seine net into the creek. She loved to follow her favorite brother Lordy and Neptune wherever they went. They were secretly pleased that she was as good as they were at almost everything.

"We already got lots of clams and oysters, and Jules says we'll have roasted oysters tonight. Too bad Mama's not here. They're her favorite the way Maum Lady fixes them!" Georgia was already thinking about wrapping some up and taking them to her mother, who opted to stay at Monticello and spend time with her baby Virginia. Little "Appy," as they called her, had proven to be a willful and spoiled two-year-old, and Anna Matilda welcomed an opportunity to dedicate some special time to her youngest.

After gathering up the shellfish and shrimp, they headed back to the house. Mary Gould and the Fraser children were excitedly waving to them from the porch.

After cleaning up, Neptune, Lordy, and Buttie helped Maum Lady and Jules roast the oysters in the back yard. They discussed the beach walk and the turtle eggs they would search for that evening.

"Miss Mary won't let us touch them, but maybe when she's not looking we can steal a couple," whispered Buttie to Neptune, looking around to make sure no one was close enough to hear him.

"Why you want dat egg, Mas' Buttie? We got de chickens fer eggs. Dem turtles come so far from dah watah to leave dere eggs; it be hard work fer 'em. We outta respect dem an' leave dem be." Neptune reproached his friend gently, reaching out and lightly punching Buttie on the arm.

At one time or another everyone had told Buttie the same thing, but he was determined that one day he would get himself a turtle egg. *Maybe even tonight, when no one's looking,* he thought. *Or better yet, I'll go back out after they've gone to bed.* He began making his secret plans. He wanted to have a turtle egg of his own.

Boyhood

Chapter Six

March 10, 1842

The boys were in Thomas Butler King's study without permission, reading through his correspondence. Just yesterday Lordy had overheard a conversation between his mother and Anne Fraser, and now he wanted to confirm the bad news himself. He asked Neptune to help him search for the document, and after a short time they found it.

Neptune, looking up from the letter, frowned at Lordy, who had already read it, and judged by his downcast eyes that he had interpreted it correctly. Both boys were very good readers for eleven years of age.

"Neptune, if Papa knew we found this letter, we'd be in big trouble. Maybe we can ask Mama some questions, but we cannot say anything to the others." Lordy leaned over him and spoke quietly and solemnly.

"Oh I knows, Mas' Lordy. I jes worried bout my family an' de oder slaves. Wat you think gonna happin' to us?"

"Nothing will happen to any of you here on Retreat. Didn't you read the part that said that all slaves 'and their increase' left to Mama by Grandpappy could not be taken away from us? You and your brothers and sisters are Sukey and Neptune's kids, so y'all will stay right here with us." Lordy tried to sound convincing. But he knew he needed his mother to explain what they had just read.

The letter they found in his father's study was his drafted

copy of a letter written in January to his creditors, confessing his inability to pay numerous debts. Some of these financial difficulties were caused by several years of poor crops, requiring expanded planting operations. Others were due to invested money in failed plans to build railroads and canals.

Now that they had returned to Retreat Plantation to live, Thomas was able to sell both his mainland properties, Waverly and Monticello. He had put one hundred slaves on the market, but had not received an adequate offer for them. Although hounded by creditors for nearly twenty years, he had been protected from financial ruin by his father-in-law's trust fund. Major William Page had left his daughter Anna Matilda the Retreat Plantation and all the original slaves, plus "their increase." In this letter, Thomas Butler King was offering to sell part of his cotton and rice business dealings, in hopes that the creditors would be flexible and work with him just a little longer.

The boys became even more worried as they read the letter. Both knew that for the last three years all the planters' cotton crop seasons were cut short due to the ravages of the caterpillar. This year's dysentery attacked many slaves and some of the planters. Lordy's parents needed to add two new wings to their simple frame house for additional family members. Virginia (Appy), John Floyd (Fuddy), and baby Richard Cuyler (Tip) had been born within the last few years, and now with nine children they definitely needed more space.

Neptune was happy that the master was home for a few months from his business and political pursuits. Miss Anna Matilda had been taking on far too much of the responsibility of running the plantation. Neptune and Lordy talked about her resentment of his father's frequent absences. They discussed how hard she worked to create the image of him as a loving, self-sacrificing father, even though he saw so little of his own children. But when Thomas Butler King was home the atmosphere was cheerful and loving, and much of the workload was taken from her shoulders.

"Papa, kin you git oder men to take away sum of de Missus's work on de plantation books?" he asked his father as they watched her work late into the night, head bent over the accounting pages.

"Son, we all try to help her, but she be one strong minded woman. She tells us ain't nobody but her an' Mausa Thomas Butler King kin work dem books," Papa Neptune assured him, shaking his head sadly.

Anna Matilda was mistress to more than one hundred enslaved men, women and children, and provided for their care with dedication and devotion. Whenever Mr. King was away, Anna Matilda cultivated the seed, supervised the planting and the construction of buildings, managed the labor force, cared for the sick, and brought crops to market. She also provided religious training for all her people, assisting her oldest daughter Tootee in teaching them Biblical lessons and scriptures. Neptune loved his mistress as he loved his own mother. He would do anything for her, and so would the other slaves.

With their heads bowed over the letter and concentrated on their discussion, the boys did not hear Anna Matilda enter the room, her long skirts trailing silently behind her.

"Here you are! What are you doing in Papa's study? What's that in your hand, Lordy?"

Lordy jumped up, embarrassed to be taken by surprise.

"Oh, Mama, we found this letter from Papa to some people he owes money to. How will Papa pay them? What will happen to us?" The earlier bravado he felt was rapidly replaced by doubt as he walked over to her and handed her the letter.

Anna Matilda turned it over to read and let out a long breath.

Eyebrows drawn tightly together, she simply said, "You boys shouldn't be worrying about adult matters. You know your Papa will always take care of us. Now scoot along, and don't be saying a word about this to your sisters and brothers. You either, Neptune. Nothing should be mentioned to your folks or any of our people." Anna Matilda admonished them sternly, her voice reproving. Yet she smiled lovingly as she watched them leave the room.

When she stood up to close the door behind them, Lordy returned to her side and lifted his fingers to her face.

"Mama, you won't tell Papa we snooped, will you?" he asked, dark eyebrows lifted in apprehension.

"Not unless the horses don't get fed and groomed, along with your other duties . . ." She sent them on their way with a grin. After watching them head toward the barn, Anna Matilda sat wearily in the nearest chair to take stock of the situation one more time. Her migraine headache had returned, and she worried at the frequency with which such maladies were affecting her.

"My family and my people will not be separated. My father's trust will be respected, and Thomas and I will do whatever is necessary to ensure that it is." She realized she was speaking willfully to herself. Despite a smile at her own silliness, a wave of immense sadness and loneliness rushed over her.

From the open doorway, Neptune watched unobserved as Anna Matilda lowered her head to her desk and allowed the tears to fall.

Chapter Seven

May 22, 1842

Neptune quivered with anticipation. Each year, at the first rumor of the drum fish's arrival, every planter on the island would ready his boats for fishing. His father Neptune, Sanders, Quamina and the other slaves who were selected for this special activity had already caulked, painted, and tarred the two Retreat boats for the season. This was the first fishing trip of the year, and both he and Lordy were invited to join them!

They had to wait for the high tide to go out, but not so far that they would be stranded in the creek, or "stuck in the cut" as his Papa called it. Master Thomas Butler King had already left for Washington City, so Quamina received permission from Miss Anna Matilda to head out shortly before the last ebb tide. Prince, Neptune, Titus, Sanders and Marcus went to row with him, but Lordy and Neptune had convinced him to include them in this early fishing expedition.

Neptune inhaled deeply, filling his nostrils with the pungent scent of jasmine. White flowers were swaying in the breeze as they boarded their boat. Traveling through the murky green waters of the river and creeks, he pointed out to his brother Sanders that the marshes and mud flats, underwater only a few hours before, had emerged between the high grounds.

"Neptune, look down yonder at the island shrinking and growing away from us," exclaimed Lordy, thrilled with the adventure of early season fishing. "But we can still see the cotton barn!" The cotton barn at Retreat, four stories tall, could be seen for many miles at sea. Some islanders told them that sailors used it as a navigational guide, along with the imposing St. Simons Island Lighthouse.

"I sees it, Mas' Lordy! My Pa sez dat on de high tides we travel much bedder dan oder times." He was charged with excitement.

Neptune turned around and watched as their tangled, shadowy, wild wood-landed island disappeared behind them. He took in the forests of live oaks draped with Spanish moss, long-leafed pine trees, and cypress and cedar lining the shores. He imagined he could still smell the fragrance of the flowers Missus Anna Matilda had planted at Retreat. As the wide stretches of beach became a distant vision, he leaned against the side of the boat and joined the others singing as they rowed.

"Knee-bone when I call you
H-a-nnn Knee-bone.
Knee-bone when I call you
H-a-nnn Knee-bone bend.
Bend my Knee-bone to the ground
H-a-nnn Knee-bone.
Bend my Knee-bone to the ground
H-a-nnn Knee bone bend.
Knee-bone in the mornin'
H-a-nnn Knee-bone bend.
Knee-bone in the evenin'
H-a-nnn Knee-bone."

The rowers sang in the odd African rhythmic cadence any group of slaves fell into no matter what the melody. When they were on their boats, the only rhythmic accompaniment would be their oars. Neptune loved this call and response singing, and had joyfully taught it to Lordy and the other King children. They sang some of these same songs on land, but the speed of the rowing version was always slower.

"Hey Neptune, how can y'all keep such good rhythm all the time?" asked Lordy.

"We jes follow de heartbeat. Is yo' pulse an' its tempo," explained Neptune with twinkling eyes.

Sanders joined in and asked him, "Doncha feel it, Mas' Lordy?"

Lordy chuckled. "I do when I'm with y'all," he answered, adding his clear tenor voice to harmonize with the song.

They rowed out to their favorite spot in the river. For the moment, all of them were united in purpose and free from the cares and distinctions of class. Neptune spotted about thirty other fishing boats riding sociably around, singing and sharing the fellowship provided by the ocean before them and the islands encircling them.

Young Neptune caught the first drum fish of the day! Soon all the fishermen brought in their share, for a total catch of nineteen fish.

As they rowed back toward Retreat Plantation, Quamina pointed out the sunset. Its flaring flames of gold and orange illuminated the marshlands, reflecting as a deep glowing red over the Frederica River.

"Dis remembahs me of de Ebo Landin'." He turned to Neptune and Sanders with an expression of deep melancholy.

Lordy picked up on the sad inflection of his remark. "What happened, Quamina?" he asked.

Quamina lowered the oar and reached over to place his large hand on his young friend's shoulder.

"It be a sad story, young Mas' Lordy." He paused for a deep breath and continued.

"A boatload of black Ebos frum Nigeria, Africa git to S'n Simons almos' at darktime many a years ago. Rat here in dis rivah at Dunbar Creek, twelve ob my folks jump over de ship an' kill theirselves, drownin' in de watah. I jes a youngin' back den. I don' wanna go wif em."

Lordy and Neptune were stunned. Neptune had heard about the Ebo Landing from his people, and the illegal practice of secretly bringing in African slaves and selling them on the island. His father told him that although slaves living in Georgia could be legally bought and sold, it had been against the law to import them from Africa for over fifty years. Still, Ebo blacks were forced onto boats in Africa and brought to Georgia, where they fetched high prices. Even knowing the story, he was completely astounded to learn that Quamina had been one of those slaves!

Lordy recovered his voice first. "But Quamina, did your people really prefer death to slavery? Would they rather kill themselves?" He shook his head in bewilderment. "And are you sorry you lived?"

The other slaves rowed in unison, humming quietly and never looking up from the water. Neptune shifted closer to Quamina to hear his answer. His heartbeat interfered with his ability to hear clearly.

"No, Mas' Lordy. I not be sorry I lib. I got good life here wif yo' family. But summa my people rader kill demselfs dan be undah bondage to oder men. Dey be chained up togetah, dey walk back in dat rivah, and dey sing 'Da watah Spirit brot me an' da watah Spirit will take me home.'"

He opened his mouth and his deep tenor voice echoed over the waters.

"Orimiri Omambala bu anyi bea.
Orimiri Omambala ka anyi ga ejina."

He sang with dignity and authority as the rowers lowered their oars. Not a sound could be heard but his song, accompanied by the quiet ripples of the water.

After a long silence Neptune spoke up. "Pa, was you dere wif Mausa Quamina?" He could hardly force his lips to ask the question.

"No, son. I come to S'n Simons frum Africa 'bout ten years latah. De Ebo Landin' happen' in 1803." His father raised his sorrowful eyes and patted Neptune's knee, smiling wistfully.

Lordy remained silent. He felt sick at heart for all the slaves. He never thought much about their feelings, believing only what he had had been told: that the slaves were protected and cared for by his family and other plantation owners. Surely they were better off under this system, he reasoned. But maybe he was living too closely to the situation to truly understand it.

As they pulled into the dock under the cover of darkness, Lordy experienced a real sense of loss and deception. Would he have the courage to die for his freedom? He glanced over at Neptune, watching him from under lowered eyelids. What about his best friend? What would he have done at Ebo Landing?

Neptune's mind was racing as he helped secure the boat. Could he even begin to comprehend the Ebo's refusal to live under bondage? Through his religious teachings, he knew that only God Himself was fit to be a master. But his Master and Missus were so kind to all of them and gave them everything they needed. Was freedom that important?

Carrying their share of the catch, the boys silently followed the men back to the house. Neptune glanced up to discover an owl smiling down at him. Just ahead of them in the forest's clearing, both boys paused to watch as two deer silently leaped in tandem and raced around the corner, disappearing into the trees.

Chapter Eight

May 23, 1842

Neptune stared out the parlor window at the resurrection ferns growing on the big oak tree. His thoughts were about the Ebo Landing story instead of the Bible study. As Tootee read 1 Corinthians 6:20, *"God paid a great price for you. So use your body to honor God,"* Quamina's words from yesterday still echoed inside his head. He wondered what he would have done. Would he have stood by watching his companions follow their chief into the depths of Dunbar Creek and drown themselves? Or would he have joined them? Was that a way to honor God?

Although Neptune understood that he and his family were the property of Thomas Butler King, he never felt like property. He loved the King family as he loved his own. They referred to him and all their slaves as "their people." Anna Matilda paid him and all the Negroes for any extra work beyond their allotted daily tasks. She paid them for the vegetables they grew on the land she lent them, for the ducks and chickens they raised on the lots behind their cabins, and for baskets and fanners they wove for her. She even lent them money to buy pigs and cows to keep for themselves or sell to other islanders or to the sailors.

How important was freedom? Their lives were good and they were protected and cared for, even into old age. He and some of the slaves on Retreat and other plantations could read and were allowed to worship their Lord whenever they wanted. Yet, in his heart, he felt that complete power over the lives of others must be against the will of God.

Neptune knew that not all slaves on coastal plantations were allowed to worship as they wished. Speaking to slaves from neighboring plantations at weddings and funerals, he learned that although they received religious instruction, it was done orally, and many were not taught to read the Bible. He knew that the slaves of Hampton Point were not allowed to leave their plantation, even to cross over Jones Creek to visit family members at Cannon's Point. Their master of many years, Major Pierce Butler, was an absentee landlord. His plantation was run by Overseer Roswell King, who was not respected or even liked by the people who lived there. Any offense they committed resulted in a whipping, paddling or loss of privileges. Sometimes this whipping was administered by the slave driver or foreman: one of their own Negroes. This demoralized the workers and encouraged deceit. Neptune had heard with his own ears the screams of agony as slaves endured whiplashes on their bare backs.

The grandson of the former master currently owned Hampton Point, and a new overseer was running it. Slaves on the island told each other that the Hampton Point slaves' lives were slowly improving.

Slavery is a Negro system of labor and a White system of command, Neptune thought to himself. *Maybe Missus Anna Matilda is right when she says it's a divine gift to the Africans and the Anglo-Saxons alike— providential. I remember when she told us in our school lessons: "The Negro came by God's command; for wiser teaching in a foreign land."*

But, Neptune thought, *if slavery is providential and wise, why are there rebellions and slave uprisings?*

His mother told him that some of Hampton Point's people

had run away and that others conspired to help them by feeding them in the woods. When they were finally captured, they were sent into solitary confinement for a short time. As far as he knew, none of the workers at Retreat Plantation had rebelled or undergone punishment. He would ask his father about that.

Is this because we're loved here? Or because our masters make us feel good about ourselves?

Although he was smart and educated, these thoughts were disturbing and difficult for an eleven-year-old boy to sort through. Something else was bothering him: something he'd been thinking about off and on since Mausa John Fraser's funeral several years ago.

The King family had attended the service at Christ Church Frederica, accompanied by Neptune and many other slaves from Retreat. All of them wanted to pay their last respects to a wonderful friend of the community. Over one hundred Negro slaves gathered in the churchyard under the shade of the great oaks, where they could hear the service and hum softly with the singing. The ceremony had ended and the slaves broke into their own buoyant, rhythmic spirituals, continuing to sing as they joined the congregation walking toward the graveyard.

"Day, day oh, see day's a com-in'
Ha'k e ang-els,
Day, day oh, see day's a com-in'
Ha'k e ang-els,
Oh, look at day, O Lord
Look out de windah, O Lord
Who dat a comin?
O Lord, look out de windah!
O Lord!"

As they sang and walked to the graveyard, some of them reflected on a strange and enticing song they had just heard, sung as a solo by a northerner. Its haunting tune and healing words transformed everyone who listened to it.

"Amazing grace, how sweet the sound
That saved a wretch like me;
I once was lost, but now I'm found,
Was blind, but now I see . . .
'Twas grace that taught my heart to fear,
And grace my fears relieved,
How precious did that grace appear
The hour I first believed.
Through many troubles, toils and snares,
I have already come;
'Tis grace hath brought me safe thus far,
And grace will take me home . . ."

Not a foot shuffled, not a throat was cleared as the words were heard and digested. Every face, dark and light, listened impassioned. They wanted to understand the meaning behind the music and lyrics.

Several weeks after the burial, Neptune and Lordy approached Miss Anne Fraser during her visit to Retreat. They sought her out, asking her to explain that unusual song that was sung at her husband's funeral.

Anne Fraser remained very quiet for a moment. Then she looked squarely into their eyes and told them.

"A dear friend explained to me that the song was written by an English clergyman named John Newton, who in his youth had been the captain of a slave ship. I believe God's grace planted those words on the heart of a man who had once made his living transporting slaves."

Then she leaned over and tenderly kissed their foreheads.

Neptune thought back to the day of the funeral. He had been closely watching the older slaves as they stood in the churchyard listening. Had he seen a look of quiet glory on the faces of his people as they assimilated the words?

Are we serving our masters without surrendering our own dignity? Perhaps we are, Neptune reasoned. *It may be possible to do so. Because real freedom is choosing who and what controls you.*

Chapter Nine

June 2, 1842

Mr. John (Jock) Couper, a longtime friend of the King family, was master of Cannon's Point Plantation. This handsome redheaded Scot was Anne Fraser's father. Growing up with the King family, he truly loved Anna Matilda and her children. Because he enjoyed horseback riding around his estate and visiting his friends across the island, he volunteered to carry the mail as St. Simon's postmaster. It was Jock who gave the King children their first ponies, during the time they were living on the mainland at Monticello. He sent one over for each of the older children, who were now outgrowing them and ready to pass them down to the smaller ones. Last week Lordy asked his parents for horses for himself, Malley and Neptune, since Tootee and Buttie already had their own.

Today the three boys were riding their ponies down to New Field, the nearby land where the field workers lived and some acres of their cotton fields were planted.

Anna Matilda asked the boys to ride over to New Field to check on the conditions of the slave quarters. The tabby cabins had windows, but no glass, so often the rainwater soaked through their makeshift barriers. Anna Matilda provided the workers with netting to keep out the mosquitoes, and checked often to be sure they were intact. She worried about pneumonia during these wet months, and today she sent the boys with new blankets and jackets for her people in New Field.

"Neptune, did you know tabby structures were used by the Indians and the Spaniards long before we were born?" asked Lordy, referring to the slave quarters, constructed of a mixture of sand, water, lime and oyster shells. Because of its strength, tabby was also used to build the slave hospitals, and the thick three-foot walls and basements of most plantations. Quamina told him that in Africa the name for this type of construction is "tabax."

"Hmm, it's sho' a good thing we learn how to make dat strong tabby, Mas' Lordy, cuz I knows for a fack dat we gonna build mo' onto de big house. I hears dat we may build anoder house for us boys!" Neptune announced with a mischievous glint in his eye.

"How come you know things about my family before I do?" asked Lordy, truly surprised.

Neptune laughed with pleasure.

"Jes sumpin' I hears, dat's all," he said with a disinterested shrug.

"Neptune, I have a question for you," announced Malley. At almost seven years, he was a precocious and often impertinent child.

"Yes, Mas' Malley. Wat you wanna axe me?"

"Since you and Sally study with us and can read so well, how come y'all talk like the others who aren't educated?" inquired Malley.

Neptune grinned over at Malley. "Dat's a good question, Mas' Malley. I knows how y'all talk an' I kin do it too. But I feel cumforble wif my dialec' cuz it's wat my folks an' my people speak. You know it cums frum my ancesters' country, Africa, an' it's mixed wif yo' English too. Dat makes me proud."

Lordy winked at him, touched by Neptune's respect for his heritage.

They rode along the soggy path, grateful for a sunny day. The last two months had been unusually wet, and besides the adverse effect on the crops, many slaves and plantation families were falling ill to "summer fever," or malaria.

As they pulled up to the slave quarters, they heard beating hooves racing down the lane behind them.

"Here cum Mausa Dunham, de Overseer. I wunder wat he wants wif us?" Neptune pulled his pony's reins short when he saw John Dunham waving wildly at them.

John Dunham reined his breathless horse in at their side. He was also breathing hard as he passed along the news.

"Boys, you'll need to hurry back to Retreat. I'll help you pass out the clothes and check the cabins, but Miss Anna Matilda needs help at the hospital. We got lots of sick people in there, and the Missus needs some extra hands. Neptune, your Mama is one of the sickly and the Missus thinks it's dysentery. She called for the doctor to come over from Darien." He was sorry to have to be the messenger of such unhappy news for Neptune.

Neptune and Lordy exchanged concerned looks and hurried to finish their chores at New Field. The lighthearted carefree moments they had just shared dissolved like the buoyant clouds hovering above only moments ago, now dark and threatening. In less than an hour the four of them pulled up to the plantation, riding at a fast pace.

As they approached the plantation from a distance, they could make out the high attic of the slave hospital, sleeping quarters for the slave women who served as nurses and midwives. The ten-room slave hospital was connected to the house by a long walk cutting through the gardens. Each room had a fireplace and two windows. The upstairs floor was for the men, while the five downstairs rooms were for the women: one for birthing and recovering, the other for sick women and children. Each of the three wards was meticulously clean and well ventilated. Anna Matilda oversaw the operation of the hospital, and often stayed there through the night when she was needed.

The boys hurried into the ward for the sick women, where they found Anna Matilda attending Clementine's youngest child, Peggy. Tootee was nearby feeding a mixture of quinine and tea to Sukey, Neptune's mother. Neptune, Lordy and Malley rushed to her bedside.

Sukey smiled weakly and patted her son's arm. "Doncha worry, dearest chile. I be sickly now but soon I be back wif y'all an' yo' Pa."

Anna Matilda gave instructions and they hurried to the kitchen to prepare more medication. There were eight sick slaves, and two women in confinement after delivering babies. All afternoon the boys, Tootee and Buttie worked closely with Anna Matilda. Dr. John Tunno arrived from Darien at sunset. After examining the patients, he sent the workers up to the house for supper and a rest.

Even the tantalizing aromas of sautéed garlic prawns and deep-fried catfish were unappreciated as they wearily collapsed at the long table to eat. All of them loved Maum Sukey and were worried about her. Before they began to eat, each one took a moment to ask God's healing powers for her and the others. Baby Tip, toddling around in his short frock, did his best to amuse them with his imitations of their voices, provoking a few distracted chuckles.

After dinner, Georgia and Flo went into the parlor to work on their studies. Tootee complained of the indigestion that often troubled her, and went to her room to sit quietly for an hour and read. Anna Matilda returned to the hospital to help out, this time refusing the boys' offer to join her.

"Enough for one day, dear hearts. Go rest, for I will need you tomorrow. Neptune, your Mama will be sleeping now, and I'll give her a kiss for you when she awakens. In the morning, first thing, you can take my place at her side." The boys knew there was no room for debate with Lordy's mother.

For the next five days at Retreat Plantation the least tired relieved the exhausted at the hospital. All of the sick eventually recovered, and Sukey was finally back on her feet and working in the kitchen. On her first day back, she found she was too weak to cook much, so Anna Matilda sat her down and took over stirring the biscuit batter. One by one the King children came into the kitchen to check on her. Neptune brought her roses, and tied a bright red one to her long black braid.

Chapter Ten

July 6, 1842

On this particular sunny afternoon, Lordy and Malley were helping Titus and Neptune groom the horses and ponies in the cotton barn, where the plantation's best horses were housed. A slight breeze wafted the fresh odors of saddle soap and polish across the stalls. Neptune breathed it in, delighting in the strong pungent mixture of salt marsh and horses' earthy fragrance. Their snorts and stomping hooves were music to his ears. Bright shafts of light flooded through the open doors, warming their arms and faces as they tended to the horses and argued about a book they were all reading.

"Hey, listen! Someone's coming," exclaimed Malley, looking up from cleaning his pony's hoof.

They heard the clip clop of several horses and exchanged surprised looks.

The horses came around the bend and the boys stared as both of their fathers approached on horseback, leading three other horses. Thomas Butler King's blue eyes twinkled and his smile was teasing.

They stopped outside the barn door.

Thomas Butler turned in the saddle to question Neptune's father. "Neptune, Sir, have the boys been compliant and hard working during my last absence?"

"Oh Yessuh, Mas' Thomas. Dey be real good boys and dey help de Missus in de hospitah fer many days," replied Neptune with a mischievous grin, displaying deep dimples on his weathered cheeks.

"Well done, lads! We think you are grown enough to care for your own horses. Come and see what just arrived from Savannah for you!" Thomas Butler and old Neptune dismounted and held out the reins to the three lads.

With hoots of delight, Lordy and Malley ran over to the black horse and the dappled mare. Neptune took a step back, and with an open mouth watched as his friends climbed into the saddles. Lordy shot an excited look over his shoulder at him.

"Neptune, get over here and look at this big beauty." He pointed to the chestnut gelding standing quietly beside him.

Neptune was speechless. This horse was so handsome it took his breath away. He approached the steed slowly, gently touching its forelock and fingering the long white mark on its nose. He marveled at the size of the horse, yet knew how fragile it was too. He rested his cheek on the gelding's silky mane.

After a few moments he recovered his voice. "You be my Chaser, purty boy. We gunna be good friends," he murmured as he rubbed the velvet nose and felt warm breath on his hand.

Lordy grinned and added, "I'm going to name mine Rocket." Turning to his father he continued. "Papa, this is so great! Thank you for these wonderful horses you brought us!" He and Malley dismounted and ran to give their father a hug.

Neptune walked over to Thomas Butler. "Yessuh, Mausa Thomas. I dunna know how to thank you. Why you git me dis hose I cain't understan', but I be grateful to you to de end of my days. Thank you." Shyly, he extended his hand to his master. Thomas Butler took it into both of his hands and squeezed it with affection. Then Neptune walked over to embrace and kiss his father.

The summer was becoming a grand season for the young men.

Chapter Eleven

July 21, 1842

It was another lazy humid summer day. Neptune and Lordy had finished their chores and it was too hot to ride. The rest of the family was resting under the cool high ceilings in the house, or sleeping in the rockers. The boys were restless and bored.

"Hey, Neptune. Do you wanna go to the beach?" Lordy thought that swimming and ocean breezes would cool them off.

"Yes, Mas' Lordy. We kin take sum fishin' stuff too fer wen it cools down," he answered.

Walking through the broad green lawn behind the house they reached a shell walk that took them through the garden and then down to the beach. Wandering through a field of golden-rods, they enjoyed the feel of the tall, flame-colored flowers reaching up to their chests. The scent of pine comforted them, with memories of carefree summers past. The ocean stretched out before them, the color of fresh-polished silver, with speckles of white froth decorating it like frosting.

It wasn't far to walk to their favorite sandy spot, where they often dribbled wet sand to create castles. The boys tossed their gear on their towels and ran into the water. The waves were gentle in low tide, so they could swim easily to the sandbar and rest. As they approached the sandbar a flock of pelicans lifted their heavy yet graceful wings in flight, circling over their heads and looking down at them as they abandoned them from above the sandbar. Several swooped into the water and surfaced with a quick afternoon snack.

The boys stretched out on the sand and watched as the tide flowed toward the land, then ebbed back past them into the sea. Their eyes took in the green and golden sea grasses that grew on the higher windblown sand dunes of St. Simons Island. Behind the spartina grass they could see twisted cedars and crooked pine trees. The upright palmettos' spongy branchless trunks and crowns of fan shaped leaves blended into the ocean scenery. The boys shared all this in a long companionable silence. Finally Lordy broke the spell.

"Hey, Neptune. John and Franny Fraser told me they saw a shark out here earlier this month."

Neptune sat up and looked out at the sea. He often saw dolphins playing close to shore, but had never seen a shark.

"Ay, I dunno. Maybe dey jes jokin' wif you. My Pa says dat de sharks only come out early mornin' an' wen it gits dark."

The waves rolled in a little rougher now. The boys got up to leave. Suddenly Lordy cried out and grabbed Neptune's arm.

"Look over there! It's a right whale breaching!" he shouted enthusiastically.

Rising with torpedo force from the water, the whale seemed to suspend itself in the air, and then smash back into the sea. As it returned to the water, its tail rose straight above the surface. When it appeared again, further out to sea, it seemed to be floating on its back, sunbathing.

"Wow!" they exclaimed, thrilled with the moment they shared, as they watched a while longer in silence.

Neptune put his hand on his friend's shoulder and walked to the edge of the sandbar.

"I'll race you!" yelled Lordy as he dove into the water.

Swimming quickly back to shore, Neptune heard a distinct

rumble even with his head under the water. He swam faster, remembering something about lightning and water. He quickly caught up with Lordy.

"It gunna rain, an' we gotta git outta de watah," he gasped as he grabbed his arm. They were near shore and could stand up now. Breathing deeply, they dragged their feet through the heavy soggy sand, trying to run, and finally hauled themselves to dry land.

Softly at first, the rain tickled the white sand, their bare backs and the sea grass. The sky darkened and cracked again as they stopped to scoop up their fishing gear and then run to the house.

The curtain of rain that fell was preceded by a roar from above. Rain poured over them as they raced, over their faces and down their bodies, so thickly they could barely see in front of them. When they wanted to say something they had to scream at each other.

Then, just as suddenly as it had begun, the rain quieted and fell more softly. The boys laughed and slowed down. A moment later, it was completely over. Slowly the sun crept back out from behind the huge clouds, which had magically turned from dark to a soft blue-gray color.

"Wow, that was amazing!" called out Lordy as he caught his breath.

On the shell walk of Retreat Plantation, they heard the songs of the spring warblers and cardinals from somewhere down the sunlit path. Nearing the formal garden, bordered by a hedge of crepe myrtle and oleanders, they were again struck by the smells of summer. The orange, lemon and date trees lifted up their light perfumes to the gentle breezes. The pungent fragrance of olive trees mingled with the sweetness of the fruits.

The scent of Anna Matilda's roses was compelling as they

neared the house. Her husband had brought her roses from all over the world, and nobody's gardens compared with these for beauty and fragrance.

Lordy turned to Neptune. "Do you remember when the captain of one of the sea vessels told Mama that he could smell the perfume of her flowers out at sea?"

"Oh, yes, Mas' Lordy. She was real happy wif him and wif Mausa Thomas fer gittin' her dem roses," grinned Neptune. He took great pride in the gardens and often helped Quamina to maintain them. Gardening was becoming more than just a hobby to Neptune. He had the knack to make things grow and an eye for beauty.

Two Persian date palms guarded the entrance to the Retreat Gardens. Neptune pointed out to Lordy the violets and snowdrops that bordered the garden beds. He showed him the new bed center, which was shaped in the form of an eight-pointed star. Anna Matilda planted a great variety of annuals, perennials and bulbs, but her favorite flower was the rose, of which she grew over one hundred varieties.

Coming around the corner to the front porch, they saw Maum Lady and Anna Matilda waiting for them, slowing swaying in the rocking chairs, towels in hand. The boys gratefully took the towels and dried off, excitedly recounting their adventures with the downpour. They stepped inside the house to a welcoming fire, and they held out their cool hands to its warmth. Anna Matilda came in and sat beside them.

"Boys, I've spoken to both your fathers about your baptisms. Pastor Stevens at the Brunswick Baptist Church will be performing two ceremonies next month, one for the white children and one for the black children. Both ceremonies will be held at Frederica River, near the fort. Neptune, Sukey and your father agree with us that you boys are old enough to be baptized and join the church, even though you are not yet twelve years old. How do you feel about it?"

"Gosh, Mama, I thought I'd be baptized with Flo in a couple of years," blurted out Lordy, interrupting Neptune's answer to his mother's question.

"Yes, that's possible. But we all thought that you boys would want to be baptized around the same time, and the preacher agreed to do both baptisms within two weeks of each other."

Lordy considered the idea. He often felt closer to Neptune than to his own siblings, and this would be something special that they would share. He decided he really liked the idea.

He looked over at Neptune. "What do you think, Neptune?" he asked hesitantly.

Neptune smiled his broad honest smile. "I be ready whenevah you be ready, Mas' Lordy."

Anna Matilda stood up and put her hand on each of their shoulders. "You boys talk it over and let us know when you come to an agreement." She smiled to herself as she walked away. Thomas was right. The boys still acted like twins.

Chapter Twelve

August 15, 1842

From the depths of the water Neptune heard the preacher's booming voice. "In obedience to the commandments of our Lord Jesus Christ I baptize thee."

Still holding his breath, he felt himself being pulled up. "In the name of the Father, the Son and the Holy Ghost, Amen."

Shivering and sputtering, he coughed and found his footing. His friend Dembo from Kelvin Grove Plantation stood next to him. He had already been baptized. On his other side, another good friend, Adam, was emerging from the water as the final words of the baptism were administered to him. Neptune looked back at the shore and saw his family and other friends waving, including the King family.

Earlier this morning all of them had walked from the church to the banks of the Frederica River, just south of Fort Frederica. The preacher, followed by his assistants, led the procession. The candidates walked behind them, girls dressed in white and boys in ordinary overalls and work shirts. Their loved ones walked behind them and made up the last part of the group.

Pastor Stevens spoke to them as they were leaving the church. "The Lord ordered us to go down into the water, so we will go to the river and hold our ceremony."

When they reached the river's edge, the pastor shared a few words of how the ceremony would take place. Prayers were offered, punctuated with encouraging responses, rhythmically delivered. The preacher walked into the river and stood in the spot selected by the deacon. An assisting deacon led each candidate into the river, where they stood next to the preacher in about two and a half feet of water. The girls' skirts were tied above their knees.

Those waiting on the shore sang spirituals during the ceremony.

"If you don' believe Ah been redeem'
Gawd's go'nah trouble duh watuh
Follow me down to Jurdun stream
Gawd's go'nah trouble duh watuh.
Wade In Nuh Watuh Children
Wade In Nuh Watuh Children
Wade In Nuh Watuh Children
Gawd's go'nah trouble duh watuh.
Who dat yonduh drest in white
Gawd's go'nah trouble duh watuh
Mus' be the childun of the Isralite
Gawd's go'nah trouble duh watuh.
Wade In Nuh Watuh Children
Wade In Nuh Watuh Children
Wade In Nuh Watuh Children
Gawd's go'nah trouble duh watuh."

Neptune watched several dozen church members singing and praying on the shore. He felt such joy seeing his sisters and brothers and parents participating. The black children were dressed in their Sunday best: the girls in calico dresses and the boys in their fanciest shirts and slacks. His sister Emiline was holding the hands of their little sisters, Mily and Linda. She blew kisses when she saw him smiling broadly. Sukey and Neptune were watching him proudly, their faces wreathed in smiles. Other plantation families whose slave children were being baptized were also there, as well as Miss Anna Matilda, Tootee, Georgia and the older King boys.

The group returned in a jubilant procession to the church, where the newly baptized children lined up to receive "the right hand of fellowship" from the preacher and church members. Neptune embraced his family; Lordy suddenly appeared alongside.

"Good work, Neptune. It wasn't too long under water, was it now?" He'd been baptized just last week, and was showing off his seniority in the matter.

"No, Mas' Lordy. I couda kept my bref even mo' time unda de watuh," replied Neptune solemnly.

The children changed into dry clothes and returned to their plantations. Neptune assisted Jimper in driving back to Retreat; Lordy and Malley rode in the back. Maum Lady was waiting for them at home, where the aromas of her delicious dinner reached their noses from the front gate. The rest of the day would be for celebration.

Neptune and Lordy went to sit on the front steps, and as they shared their experiences, they suddenly felt older and special. They had been told that Christ lived within them, and today they were sharing this blessing. Later, Neptune's eyes glowed with happiness as he sat with the King family at the dinner table.

Chapter Thirteen

September 26, 1842

"Boys, would you like to go fishing on the mainland with us for the next few days?" Thomas Butler suggested, with a twinkle in his eyes.

"Yes Papa, you know we would!" they yelped gleefully.

"Then get Neptune and his Papa and let's plan a trip!"

It was always a special occasion when the boys accompanied the adults on a fishing trip to the mainland, but especially when Thomas Butler joined them. This time they would spend the first night with one set of friends, fish the following day, stay over with another family that night, fish half of the third day and return late in the evening to their island. There was nothing in this world that Neptune, Lordy and Buttie liked to do better!

The four rowers included Quamina and big Neptune, who would also be their fishing guides. As they left the dock, Buttie, Lordy, and Neptune relaxed in a thirty-foot long canoe hollowed out of a cypress tree. They were lulled by the gentle rhythm made when the oars lapped the dark waters. Happily they accompanied the black oarsmen as they eased into their improvised song.

"Do Lord, do Lord, do ya remember me?
Way over in Geojah land?
Do Lord, do Lord, do ya remember me, oh yeah!"

Lordy nudged the others to look back at Retreat. Georgia, Flo and Appy were running down to the dock to wave goodbye. As they pulled around the bend and out of sight, they turned back to admire the beauty of the massive live oak forest, twisted cedars, crooked pines and upright palmettos. Sometimes, when the rowers moved in perfect unison, it almost felt like the canoe was lifting off the water.

"Listen! Can y'all hear the palmettos rattling like bones in the wind?" asked Lordy, an avid reader who loved to show off his literary knowledge.

Buttie sneered and answered sarcastically. "Certainly, my lord. And do watch for amphibious creatures, serpents and great-winged fowl soaring above!"

The rowers looked up from their singing and smiled. The boys bantered throughout the trip and spoke with enthusiasm of the adventure awaiting them. Although they enjoyed fishing in their creeks and smaller rivers, the Altamaha River was enormous, full of shoals, banks, mud and sand bars. Just the sort of challenge that boys their age welcomed!

Neptune relaxed and daydreamed about the raccoon and opossum hunting last week. Master Thomas Butler King had given each son a new hunting rifle in late August. The boys practiced shooting with Overseer Dunham and Neptune's father, and finally were allowed to go on a "critter hunt." They had no luck with the crafty opossums but finally chased a raccoon up a tree.

"Take good aim, boys. Get a clear view of him and look him in the eye before you shoot." Overseer John Dunham coached the three boys and then stepped back.

"Go, Mas' Lordy. Shoot first!" encouraged Neptune.

"You shoot, Buttie." Lordy's voice came out between a croak and a whisper.

Buttie shot and missed, startling the raccoon further up the tree. The boys put down their rifles and discussed strategy. After several minutes, the raccoon retraced its steps back to one of the lower branches, sensing the danger had passed.

"Who wanna try dis time?" asked Neptune's father. "Now be good time cuz he's tire' an' trustin' in us."

Neptune was surprised when Lordy handed him his rifle. "This one is for you, Neptune. You shoot!"

He relived his words to his mother afterward, savoring the moment.

"I done de bes' I could, Mama. Dere dat coon was, settin' where I lef 'em. I put my gun on him, shot ' em b'tween de eyes, an' he fell outta de tree, kerplunk onto de ground. Ain't dis as fine a coon as you evah seen?"

Sukey assured him it was indeed the most beautiful one she'd ever had the opportunity to cook, and they enjoyed a special raccoon stew later that night. The memory brought a huge grin to Neptune's lips. Buttie nudged him to ask what he was thinking.

"Hmm, Mas' Buttie. I jes rememberin' dat coon huntin' trip, dat's all."

"Yeah, we gotta do that again. Papa, can we go next week and try to get opossum too? Maybe even over on the mainland, when they have the hunt with the horses and the dogs!" Buttie loved activities on the mainland. Neptune wondered if it was because of the young ladies who lived over there.

"Maybe in a few weeks, son," answered Thomas Butler King. "I've got work to get done next week. But we'll do it before I leave Retreat."

Approaching the mainland dock, Neptune thought about his friend, Ila. She was the daughter of a blacksmith who lived on Hopeton Plantation near Brunswick. Jock Couper's son, James Hamilton Couper, was the owner of Hopeton. Neptune met Ila at a funeral on St. Simons Island where they discovered they had some relatives in common. She was lively and pretty and made him laugh.

Who knows, maybe I'll even meet her again on this trip, he thought as he fought the temptation to doze off.

A loud voice jolted him back to reality. "Hey Neptune, give me a hand with the ropes. We got some fishin' to do!" Lordy tossed him the rope, splashing water across his cheeks and shirt. Shaking his head and laughing, Neptune scooped up a handful of water and tossed it back. Time for another adventure!

Chapter Fourteen

January 15, 1845

For weeks the King household had been preparing for the upcoming nuptials. Tootee, the oldest King child, was marrying William Couper. He was her childhood friend and teenage sweetheart, and the youngest brother of Anna Matilda's dear friend, Anne Couper Frazer. The dresses and suits for the wedding party had been ordered from Savannah, Georgia and London, England. For weeks the women from the other plantations had worked side by side with Anna Matilda and her slaves: spinning cotton and cutting and sewing the servants' outfits for this very special event. The festivities, which would begin at the home of the bride and end at the home of the groom, called for tremendous preparation.

The King family followed tradition by bringing Tootee's husband an entire household of furnishings that they had been collecting since her birth.

"Mama, are you saving something for me when I marry?" worried Tootee's younger sister, Georgia.

"Of course we are, dearest. And your sisters will have their dowries also. It's just that this is the first time any of you has married. It does seem overwhelming, doesn't it?" She kissed her daughter on the top of her head. Anna Matilda was always careful to smooth over the ruffled feathers of her children.

The family's out of town relatives had arrived during the last several days to help Anna Matilda and Thomas King with final details. Her neighbors also helped Anna Matilda make wedding decorations to place in her home and in Christ Church Frederica. For a centerpiece on her long dining table, she asked the carpenters to make small wooden Gothic temples of love, which were later decorated with flowers and evergreens. A lighted candle placed in the middle would be lit during the wedding dinner at Retreat Plantation.

Satin ribbons and streamers, as well as other adornments, were purchased from Yankee peddlers in their gaily-painted mule-drawn wagons. Thomas Butler King had recently returned from Savannah, his schooner laden with everything on her long shopping list.

Anna Matilda's people were very happy to help her. They loved Tootee and had known William since his birth. Their "Missus" insisted on paying them for this extra work, but young Neptune flatly refused.

"Missus, you aways treat me lika yo' son an' I won't take no money fer helpin' Miss Tootee on her happies' day."

Anna Matilda smiled fondly. Just yesterday Anne Fraser had told her that their people mirror them faithfully, and Neptune was proving her correct.

"Neptune, I declare that you know me better than I know myself! What a beautiful gift you are giving to Tootee: your love and devotion."

"It allus make Neptune glad to be doin' fer you, Missus Anna." Neptune gave her his heartfelt wide smile and softly left the room.

He hurried to the carriage house, checking to be sure the horses were ready and the carriages decorated. For the very first time, Jimper was letting him drive one of the carriages. He would be driving Tom and Jerry to transport the family to the wedding. He checked to make sure that all the carriage horses were brushed and fed before they were taken out. In the past, he had assisted Jimper and Sam in driving the carriages, but today he would drive solo, as a surprise to Tootee and her family. Naturally Lordy knew of his plan, but no one else besides Jimper, Sam, and Frederic, the three slaves who drove and cared for Retreat's harnesses and carriages, expected Neptune to drive one of the bride's family carriages to the church.

Fortunately, this winter had been mild. The sun streaked across the sky as the wedding party finished their preparations at the house. Neptune and the drivers lined up the carriages to transport them to Christ Church Frederica. Pleased and surprised to see Neptune driving, Anna Matilda waved to him.

"You look so handsome Neptune. Wait 'til the children see you driving!"

She turned to Thomas, draping her arm softly over his.

"Dearly beloved, I can hardly believe this. Look at us! I remember so well our own nuptials, and now we're giving away our oldest daughter in marriage." She looked into his bright blue eyes; her dark eyes shone with love.

"Yes, my sweet lady. It is Tootee's time, and we'll be doing this again and again, until all remaining eight are wed."

Anna Matilda thought fleetingly of their little William Page, now in Heaven with the angels.

She looked down as their second youngest, John Floyd (Fuddy), only five years old, entered the room. *Would they still be here for his wedding?* she wondered, sighing softly.

Thomas Butler looked into her eyes and lifted her chin. "You are so lovely. You could be the bride yourself," he whispered as he kissed her lips.

It is time to move on, thought Anna Matilda with sudden joy. *My little Hannah Page King will become Mrs. William Couper this very day!*

Chapter Fifteen

January 15, 1845

For the next hour the King family arrived at the church in carriages that moved back and forth along the path from Retreat to Christ Church. Many slaves from other plantations were granted permission to join their masters, so the grounds quickly filled up with people eager to celebrate the blessed event. After stepping out of their carriages, the plantation owners moved to benches under the trees to receive their mail from Jock Couper. The postmaster used any social engagement to distribute the letters and packages that reached the island. As they read their mail and discussed the latest news, their children played noisily under the shaded oaks, and the ladies gathered inside the church for gossip. When the Reverend E. P. Browne pronounced the words "Dearly beloved," it was time to begin the ceremony.

With the guests finally seated, the organ music commenced inside the church. Neptune hurriedly finished helping Lordy and his brothers into their dress suits, very similar to the groom's, and then went to sit with his family at the back of the church.

William Couper stood at the altar, looking around nervously for his bride. He was dressed in a black evening suit with a swallow-tailed coat, white vest, white silk necktie and white kid gloves. He painted a handsome picture with his blond hair, blue eyes, tall physique and fair complexion. In contrast, lovely Tootee King stood in the doorway of the church, dark black hair shining under her veil, her intelligent brown eyes glowing with excitement. As the bridesmaids walked up the aisle with the groomsmen, she turned to wink at old Neptune and Sukey. Young Neptune blew her a kiss, and then closed his eyes in a silent prayer of thanksgiving.

Miss Hannah Page King walked slowly down the aisle, her hand tucked under her father's arm, smiling at everyone who met her eyes. She radiated happiness and high fashion in her lovely dress made of white crepe de Paris, with its handsome wide brocade silk sash. The full skirt flounced up to her waist. The tulle veil, bordered with lace and a wreath of orange blossoms, fell to the edge of the skirt and enveloped all of her but her face.

Tootee enhanced her outfit with white kid gloves and silk boots and a saucy crepe bonnet, trimmed with delicate pink and white flowers. Her long gold earrings gleamed as the sun streamed through the bright hues of the stain-glassed windows of Christ Church.

"Will you take this woman to be your lawfully wedded bride?" she heard Rector Browne's voice from the distant chambers of her mind.

"I will!" answered William distinctly.

When it was her turn, Tootee, never at a loss for words, heard her heart beating out of control and could only nod her assent.

They exchanged rings. William had made her one with their initials engraved around a heart. She gave him an elegant gold ring with a cornelian stone.

As they walked arm in arm out the church's front doors and into the fresh garden air, they were greeted by servants singing harmoniously in clear voices. Jock Couper had convinced his fiddler Johnny to put on a kilt and play the bagpipes, much to the delight of everyone present—his surprise gift to the bride and groom!

Neptune smiled as he drove the family members back home, then returned for more people. This was such an honor for him. Both Tootee and William had complimented him on his demeanor as he drove them back home. Later, driving the King boys home, he joyfully discussed the ceremony with his friends.

"Johnny sho' played dem bagpipes nice, didn't he?" Neptune spoke with pride.

"Yes he did! Who even knew that ole Jock would teach him to play for Tootee's wedding! I think that was the best part of it all," answered Malley.

"And look at how handsomely you drive Tom and Jerry," teased Lordy, tugging the edge of Neptune's ear.

"Nah, it's deese horses dat draws real fine. Deys de gayest movers I ever see an' so gentle too, but still full of life," said Neptune, pleased with the compliment.

"Hey, you're too modest, Neptune." Buttie had always admired that quality in Neptune. As they reached their front porch he exclaimed, "And now comes the best part: the banquet at our house!"

Neptune thought the guests gathering in the parlor and dining areas of Retreat were so elegant. The men were in ruffled shirts fashioned from the best linen, under coats of soft velvet. The women looked splendid in their imported silks and satins, styled into lovely gowns. Neptune also was dressed in his best outfit: a black evening suit with vest and a necktie. For the first time, he felt completely grown-up.

Pound cake and iced tea were served upon arrival at Retreat Plantation, with groomsmen helping the waiters serve the ladies. The men smoked and drank brandy, while the women mingled and shared the latest news. At ten o'clock in the evening, dinner was announced. The wedding couple sat down at the head of the table, while the guests gathered around them.

The ladies ate first and the gentlemen later conducted them back to the parlor. Then they returned to serve themselves.

The dining table was heaped with food for over one hundred guests. One end was piled with cold sliced turkey, hot roasted beef and pork, and smoked tongue of beef. Breads, biscuits and garden vegetables were set in the middle of the table. At the far end were pickles, jellies, pound cakes, fruitcakes, ice cream, gelatin, candies and tropical fruits. Wines, whiskeys and brandies were served throughout the meal.

Shortly after dinner, the music struck up for dancing. Young and old joined in and danced minuets, gigs, reels, waltzes and country dances. Banjos and fiddles and even the bagpipes accompanied the singing voices to the beat of drums and the harmonica. The dancing continued well into the morning hours.

Neptune was enjoying himself waltzing with his pretty girlfriend Ila. She worked in the rice fields on the mainland, and they had known each other for several years. Even though they only met at festivities and funerals, their relationship was growing into something special for them both. As fireflies lit their silhouettes on the dark porch, he held her closely and whispered into her ear how well she danced. She blushed and told him that it was only because he knew how to lead her so well. Quite unexpectedly, Neptune experienced a feeling of peace flowing through him as he held Ila in his arms.

Finally, in the early hours of the morning, the party wound down and families gathered to drive home. Neptune watched with regret as Ila rode away to return to the mainland.

The party continued the following day with a big picnic at Retreat. Tootee and William stayed around for the fun. The bride's "second day" dress was almost as important as her wedding dress. She walked through the garden splendidly dressed in a light blue silk gown. Then the third day they moved the activities to the groom's house, where the bridal couple joined them once again. Tootee and William stayed on the island for an entire week. They finally boarded the stage, almost reluctant to leave their families to honeymoon in Savannah.

After their farewells, Anna Matilda turned to her husband.

"May we both live to see each of our children as joyously married as Tootee!" Thomas King squeezed her hand in agreement.

Neptune and Lordy exchanged knowing looks, raised their eyebrows and stifled their giggles. Pleased with the idea, each one wondered how his wedding would be.

Chapter Sixteen

February 28, 1846

Neptune's horseshoe clanked noisily against the post. He turned to Lordy and Malley with an enthusiastic shout. "Ringer!"

"Dat's de game boys," he grinned broadly, animated by the win.

Lordy and Malley walked over to verify and conceded the match. As they were speaking, a short, loud toot of the conch broke into their conversation.

The boys were playing horseshoes on the lawn of Grasshopper Hall, the new addition to their house. This two-story tabby cottage, attached to the main house by a breezeway, was built to give privacy and ample living quarters to the older King boys. It had quickly become a favorite place for their friends to meet. Fun loving Fuddy had named it Grasshopper Hall when he was just five, having discovered the leaping insects living under the construction site as the addition was being built.

The boys listened to the repeated tooting of the conch.

"How strange," murmured Malley. "It's not a call for help, and no one is expected to visit today. So why do you think they're calling us?"

"Since it's the 'hurry, hurry' signal, I'm guessing that it has something to do with Tootee's baby," said Lordy.

"Dat's true! She be havin' her baby 'bout now, I reckon!" Neptune brushed the dirt from his clothes and hurried back to the main house with the others following closely behind.

Entering through the back door of Retreat, they were met by Maum Lady, wearing a delighted smile on her weathered face.

"Missus Tootee was jes delivered of a lil' girl this mornin', and she be called Anna lik yo' mama!"

"That's great, Maum Lady! Who rode over to tell us? How did you find out? How's Tootee doing? Where's Mama?" Buttie's questions tumbled out in rapid succession.

"You know yo' mama hassa be wif Missus Tootee at Hamilton Plantation. She send her best an' dat blessed news wif Marcus, who be in de kitchen rat now. You kin axe him yo' questions if you wish." She smiled at their excitement and protective love for their sister.

"Hey, let's ride over to see them now!" suggested Lordy. "Then we might could see Mama and Georgia too."

Neptune, Buttie, Lordy and Malley saddled up their horses and rode over to visit their sister. As they traveled the familiar trail, they passed their friend and Tootee's brother-in-law, James Hamilton Couper. He congratulated them on the birth of baby Anna, reported that everyone was well, and continued on his ride.

"James Hamilton is always the gentleman, isn't he?" noted Malley with admiration. "Sometimes he seems older than his dad, ole Jock."

"Yeah, and he's an excellent businessman. He always has money for his business ventures and is willing to lend it to help others, too." Lordy spoke warmly of their friend.

"Do y'all remember back a few years, when we lost Waverly and Monticello and some of our people to Papa's creditors? Mama was so unhappy losing Davy and Richard and Peggy and the others that she borrowed several thousand dollars from James Hamilton to buy them back when they were sold at Marshal's Auction. He's always helped us out, and now he's making sure that Tootee's William is making wise investments." Buttie, who had a keen business mind, was eager to learn from successful businessmen.

Reaching Tootee and William's home at Hamilton, where William worked as plantation manager, they ran up the porch and hurried inside. The smell of fresh-baked lemon pound cake wafted all the way from the pantry to the parlor. Georgia greeted them joyfully and joined them, serving them tea and some still warm pound cake. Anna Matilda heard them below and came quickly down the stairs, eager to show off her first grandbaby Anna. The tiny baby was a bundle of pink and white skin, wrapped up in a soft yellow blanket. Each boy took turns holding her for a few moments, before hurrying upstairs to see their sister and brother-in-law.

Tootee, in spite of her frequent poor health, glowed with happiness. She received them, propped up by feather pillows and sitting up in bed.

"Hey, it was easy," she beamed. "Little Anna really wanted to come into the world, and arrived quickly. Mama and Maum Lady were with me all the time, and Georgia got here in the middle of it all. I'm just fine, really." She smiled confidently at her husband, squeezing his hand.

"I'm happy you two named her after Mama," said Malley. "She must be real pleased."

"Yes, Missus Tootee. Dat be de nicest thing you do fer yo' Mama. And she deserve it mo' den anyone, I reckon'." Neptune handed her the flowers he and Malley had stopped to pick for her on the ride over.

"Thank you so much, Neptune. You always remember the details. It looks like it's finally rubbing off on these brothers of mine." She teased.

After a hearty dinner of English prawns, fried green tomatoes and drum fish, the boys prepared for the ride home. Anna Matilda promised to return to Retreat for a short visit in a day or two, and Georgia told them she would ride back the next day to take over the Mistress duties on the plantation. Each one held little Anna one more time and told Tootee that they would all come back soon. This baby was their first niece, and each one of them was already feeling a special place in his heart for her.

Chapter Seventeen

March 30, 1846

Neptune, Buttie, Lordy and Malley were astride their horses riding sleepily to Cannon's Point on the north end of the island. Bundled up in warm clothing to combat the early morning chill, they laughed when their horses' breaths fogged over their noses with every snort. As Neptune warmed his hands under Chaser's thick mane, he relished his horse's heavy streams of breath warming his cheeks.

The sun was just beginning to rise, promising warmth and adventure for the new day. They rode slowly through the dark forest and watched in wonder as the colors of the sky changed from a deep purple rose to an ashen rose, and then to pink and mauve. In less than an hour they would meet up with Jock and William Couper for some early morning deer hunting. Anna Matilda trusted them with her dear friend Jock, aware that all four boys were sharp shooters and responsible hunters.

As they wound their way through the forest near Lawrence Plantation, their thoughts were interrupted by a squirrel scurrying across the road, barely escaping the horses' hooves. He crossed over the path and scampered halfway up a gum tree, then sat scolding them from a branch, flicking his tail back and forth through the early sunlight.

Just then, frantic screams broke the morning silence and frightened a great blue heron to lift her heavy wings in hurried escape from the branches of a gnarled old oak.

The distant tormented cries were repeated, and were unmistakable. Someone was getting a lashing. The whistles of the whip followed by screams were heartrending. The boys reined in their horses and sat in shocked disbelief.

Finally Lordy spoke out. "That damn Roswell King must be whipping his slaves at Hampton Point!" His face was red with fury and he was outraged at the cruelty. "What's wrong with that man? Why is he so terrible to his people?"

Neptune shook his head and reached forward to comb his fingers through Chaser's mane. "Sumbody must hab cross Jones Creek to visit family ober dere. An' dey get caught."

"I hate that! He's the only overseer who whips his people around here! Can't we do something about it? I can't believe that Mama was born on that slave-beating plantation! I know that was during the time that Major Pierce Butler still lived there, but I wish he could see what's happening on his property!" Malley's voice cracked with unbridled indignation.

"All mausas ain't made wif de same hearts, Mas' Malley. My people be lucky to b'long to yo' papa, Mausa King, wif no whippin' allow. If we steals or sasses or does sumpin' bad, we hafta do wifout sumpin' we like fer a spell. But dem po' people hab diffrent crosses to carry."

Lordy nodded sharply and urged Rocket forward as the others gradually followed. The rest of the ride to Cannon's Point passed in grim silence.

Jock and William Couper were waiting for them in front of their plantation, saddled up and eager to begin the hunt. As they galloped back into the forest, all tormenting thoughts of the beating were momentarily set aside. The feeling of the energy of one of God's most powerful creatures beneath them, yielding to their human's commands with willing devotion, gave them the enormous sense of freedom they craved.

By noontime, the hunters had returned to Cannon's Point with two large bucks. William and Buttie were the fortunate ones who had sighted and shot them. The servants immediately began to field dress the deer, gutting them and draining their fluids. Then they would hang them up to cure for a week. One of Jock Couper's people would eventually cut them into smaller pieces and carry Buttie's deer on horseback to Retreat for the King family to enjoy.

Before the meal, the guests were served the whiskey or brandy of their choice. Only Buttie accepted this beverage and joined the others, who sat around conversing and drinking sweetened tea. After briefly talking over current political events with them, Neptune excused himself and went to eat in the kitchen with his slave friends.

By one o'clock, everyone was seated at the large Couper table enjoying dinner. Jock Couper had the best cook on the island: Cassamene Sans Foix, a colored free man from Santa Domingo who had once worked for Mr. Thomas Spalding on Sapelo Island. During a visit to Thomas Spalding's home, Jock tasted the delectable meals Mr. Sans Foix prepared. Standing in front of his good friend Thomas, Jock had boldly offered Mr. Sans Foix double his salary to come work with him. Sans Foix agreed, and everyone quickly discovered that he was worth it.

Sans Foix could de-bone a whole turkey and still maintain the roasted bird's original shape. He never allowed anyone to see how he did it. If one dared to enter the kitchen during the process, Sans Foix placed a spotless white cloth over the turkey, concealing the mystic rite as he continued his work. Today he and his assistant, Cupidon, welcomed the King boys as they served them one of their typical, exquisite dinners. Guests were beckoned to dinner by Johnny's bagpipes.

Today the table was set as always with beautiful Irish linen. A great ham of bacon sat at the head of the table. A delicious saddle of mutton weighed down the other end. Between them, Sans Foix personally scattered an enticing diversity of poultry and fried chicken. The boys were overcome by engaging aromas as they sat down at the table.

A profusion of products from the garden was placed in the center of the table. The guests could also select oysters or crabs, as well as pickles of every kind and color. Dinner wines were offered in an almost frozen state. Finally, rich chocolate and lime desserts added a finishing touch to the meal.

The King boys and Neptune were completely satisfied after such a sumptuous dinner. Each one secretly wanted to nap, but they knew their ride home was long and soon darkness would fall. With heartfelt thanks to Jock Couper and his staff, they straddled their now well-rested and well-fed mounts and headed for home.

"That was indeed one of the most pleasant days I've ever had," declared Buttie as they trotted away from Cannon Point. "Jock Couper is certainly one grand fellow. And a great family friend as well!"

"Look at de sunset!" exclaimed Neptune. "It sho' be purty dis evenin'."

They watched the sun spreading across the late afternoon, setting the top of the orchard on fire while darkness strained to collect underneath. Finally, the redness seeped from the day and night emerged.

When she heard the galloping hooves signal their arrival, Anna Matilda hurried to light up the darkened doorway and welcome her boys home. From a distance they could see her standing on the front porch, dressed in spotless white, her cap gleaming like snow on a sunlit mound.

Chapter Eighteen

November 21, 1848

Neptune knew that Ila was his lifetime companion. Tonight he would be back on the mainland and they would be together again. Miss Anna Matilda was sending him over there to pick up supplies, knowing full well that there would be a wedding on Hopeton Plantation where Ila lived. He loved his Missus for her keen intuition.

His boat moved with a steady, rocking motion as he rowed to the south branch of the Altamaha River. Singing along with the rhythm of the oars, he looked up to see James Hamilton Couper's stately mansion rising on fertile land beside the broad canal. Moving closer to shore, he began searching his mind to remember how old he was when he met Ila. He laughed out loud as he realized that he already knew her when he was baptized at almost twelve years of age. Her image was foremost in his mind as he was dunked under the water. So they probably met at a summer party the year before at Hamilton Plantation.

Over the years they continued to see each other at weddings, funerals, parties and sometimes at church functions. Both of their masters were gracious about allowing their slaves to attend functions away from their plantations.

The older King boys teased him about his infatuation for Miss Ila. They met and flirted with many young women, forgetting them quickly when new ones were presented to them. Neptune was different. From the first moment he met Ila, he knew she was special in the way that older men would know.

She was very attractive, with short curly dark brown hair and copper skin, but she was also self-assured, which left a strong impression on his young mind. She walked with grace and seemed to mysteriously light up the room when she entered. Her smile was slow and contagious, and it warmed his heart.

And she was very brave. Several years ago they attended a large picnic at Hamilton Plantation. A few of the younger slaves walked down to the creek to skip rocks and exchange plantation news. Ila was walking over some mossy boulders, holding tightly to Neptune's hand to keep from slipping. He remembered that she suddenly let go of his hand and bent over.

"Ooohh, whew," she exhaled softly and moaned.

"Ila, what's wrong?" Neptune was anxious with worry.

"Someting bit me an' it hurt real bad," she whimpered, reaching for her foot.

Neptune looked behind them and saw a scorpion scurrying away. He grabbed a large rock and threw it with all his might, crushing the insect on the spot. Then he turned around and knelt before Ila.

Pulling his pocketknife from his pants, he gently probed into the red swelling skin on her foot to open the wound. Calling to the others to bring up water, he cleaned it out, speaking slowly and gently to her the whole time.

"Ila, dis will sting fer a bit, but we gunna wash summa de poison out now. Den I gunna take you back to de house an' we git de medicine you need."

Ila nodded her consent, and bit her trembling lip. Neptune and a friend formed a chair with their hands and carried her back to the plantation house. She smiled her fragile sweet smile even as she fought back tears.

After she was placed on the bed, a nurse was summoned to care for her wound. She cleaned it out with soap and water and placed a cold compress over it. Then she gave Ila some healing roots to chew on as she elevated the foot, and made her a strong bitter tea to drink.

Neptune stayed by her side, rubbing her forehead and soothing her with his comforting words. Her dark eyes observed him closely, radiating appreciation.

As Neptune thought back on that day, he decided that was the day he knew she would be his sweetheart. They were probably fourteen years old then. Several weeks later, he shared his feelings for her with Lordy.

"Neptune, how can you know she'll be your girl forever? You'll meet lots of other women in your lifetime." Lordy was surprised and a little envious.

"I jes knows, dat's all. To me it's a fack dat my brain tells my heart," answered Neptune, smiling with conviction.

"Okay my friend, we'll talk in five years," answered Lordy, his eyes twinkling with amusement.

More than three years had passed and Neptune cared for Ila with a deep commitment. He wasn't sure that she felt the same way, because they had not yet spoken of love. But every time he saw her, she awarded him her time and attention. Tonight would be another opportunity to learn more about each other. It had been four months since he'd seen her, and he was both apprehensive and excited.

He docked the boat and hurriedly completed the errands Miss Anna Matilda had sent him to do. Since he would be spending the night with some friends at Hopeton Plantation, he went over there to clean up and dress for the wedding. He had not yet seen Ila.

The wedding was held in a small chapel near Hopeton Plantation. Neptune looked around as he entered, and immediately spotted Ila sitting with her parents up front. The bride was her cousin and he knew they were part of the wedding party. He sat in the back of the chapel and waited with excitement for the ceremony to finish.

As the bride walked up the aisle, Ila turned to watch her and saw Neptune. A warm smile spread slowly across her face and she blushed, her skin tingling. Neptune noticed and was giddy with happiness. Boldly, he winked and raised his hand in a return greeting. He was delighted when she looked down at her hands.

The party was held in the fields of Hopeton Plantation. By the time Neptune arrived with his friends, the music had already begun. He walked up to Ila and gave her a hug.

"Miss Ila, you sho' look beautiful tonite," he began. "I be honored to dance wif you." Without waiting for her answer, he took her hand and led her to the dance floor.

Neptune never left her side from that moment on. They shared dinner, laughed through the festivities, danced only with each other, and sat quietly by themselves under an oak tree draped with gray Spanish moss. Neptune decided to tell her what he was thinking.

"Ila, we bin good friends fer mo' den four years now. You be real special to me an' I wanna axe you to be my gal. How you feel bout me?"

Ila lowered her beautiful chestnut eyes and squeezed his hand. "Neptune, I always care fer you since I meet you. You be wat I look fer in a man. Nobody else is like you fer me. I already tell my folks dat a long time ago." She smiled, lowering her eyes.

Neptune leaned forward and lifted up her chin. Then he raised her lips to his. Softly and firmly, he kissed them. Ila let him, closing her eyes. When she opened them again she reached for his hands.

"I wait fer you here in Hopeton. We see each oder wen we kin. It be fine dat way, Neptune. Doncha worry none bout me."

Neptune closed his eyes and said a silent prayer. He could not believe his good fortune. *No, my blessings*, he decided. *Thank you, Lord. This is a gift from Heaven.*

The night drew to a close. Neptune and Ila said goodbye once more, and promised to see each other at the next opportunity.

This time, thought Neptune as he rowed back to Retreat Plantation, *I will convince Lordy that I am the luckiest man on earth.* He smiled broadly and shouted with joy as he rounded the bend and saw the lighthouse of St. Simons Island saluting him in the distance.

Chapter Nineteen

June 3, 1850

Neptune and all the other available slaves on St. Simons Island were staying in the slave quarters at Hamilton Plantation to help care for the injured. Mausa William Couper had turned the second floor of his barn into a temporary hospital for burn victims and was laboring long hours, in addition to running errands for the doctors who came over from Darien and Brunswick to help. Neptune admired the strength and endurance of Mausa William and Miss Tootee. They were ceaselessly working through the crisis, even though they now had three small children to attend.

It had been a terrible, ghastly accident. During its run from Savannah to Florida, the steamboat Magnolia stopped two days ago at Hamilton's dock to load cotton and pick up a few passengers traveling south. Just as the people were boarding, unpacking their trunks and settling in, the peaceful coastal ambiance was cut short by a terrible "BOOM!" that reverberated through the silent air as the boiler exploded. Witnesses recalled the horrific sight of unfortunate passengers and freight being hurled in every direction.

Neptune grieved with the others as they cared for the terribly burned survivors. Many lives were lost. Days later servants and family members continued to find bodies washed up on the shores of the tributaries. Neptune wept angrily and unashamedly when he came across the burned corpse of his good friend Dembo.

The King family lost all the cotton they had loaded on the Magnolia to be sold in Florida. But much worse, they lost the two slaves who were loading it. Miss Anna Matilda broke down in tears when she was notified. She sent all her slaves who were willing to help over to Hamilton to help her daughter and son-in-law. Neptune and his father were the first to arrive. When they reached Hamilton, they immediately began to cut open bales of cotton to make beds for the burn victims.

Neptune was anxious and melancholy as he made the bales as comfortable as possible for the patients. Reliving the past six months, he found himself feeling sad as well as bitter.

His "twin" Lordy had been away at Yale University, studying undergraduate work and rooming with Hamilton Couper, Jock's grandson. Although he often sent letters to Missus Anna Matilda and to him, Neptune missed the closeness they shared and was beginning to feel so far removed from Lordy's life. Now the family and some of his friends began calling Mas' Lordy "Lord," which seemed so unfamiliar to Neptune's mind. He decided in quiet defiance to always call him Lordy.

Last week he received a depressing letter from Lordy written from Washington City. In the letter Lordy reflected on his pain and sadness upon learning about the death of Mausa Jock Couper, who had died on March 24, 1850. Lordy was very upset that he could not be home for the funeral, because he was the only King child who did not attend. Neptune missed him very much at the funeral. He understood that for several weeks Lordy had been accompanying his father on an important political assignment and couldn't make it home, but it frustrated him just the same.

Sometimes I feel freer than the King sons, Neptune thought. *I learned from the Bible that Paul says we are all bondservants in Christ. I am bound to Mausa King and Missus Anna Matilda through slavery, but the boys are bound through duty and obedience. The Bible tells us we are to be broken bread and poured out wine. Yet we are all free to love our Lord, and all are created to serve. Before Him, our lot is equal.*

Neptune still struggled with his feelings about the inherent wrongness of slavery. Sometimes he discussed it with his family, and concluded that their lot was probably better than others. He felt duty bound to be with the King family.

Neptune worried about Mausa Thomas Butler King. Lordy and Buttie had explained over the years that their father was a visionary: a man who dreamed large and tried to make things happen. He knew that Mausa King was one of the first men to envision the transcontinental railroad; he helped put Georgia ahead of any other state in the Union back in 1843 when they laid thirty-six miles of track. His plan was to run the course from Brunswick, Georgia to San Diego, California. Somewhere along the way, and after years of effort, that project fizzled and failed.

Thomas Butler King was later elected to the U.S. Congress as a representative from Glynn County and quickly caught the eye of the President of the United States. When Lordy returned home in August of last year he explained to Neptune the importance of President Zachary Taylor's commission that had just been given to his father.

"Neptune, this is Pa's big opportunity! The President has appointed him to visit California as his advisor to check on the conditions among the Indians. But Papa believes that his true mission is to present President Taylor's dream that California will apply for statehood soon. He feels that the new state will be sympathetic to slavery and perhaps support the south." Lordy's face beamed with pride at the thought that his father would soon acquire credibility and fame. Surely that would get them all out of debt.

"Mas' Lordy, I hopes you be right. De factors are pressurin' yo' Mama fer money an' she needs sum peace an' security round here," answered Neptune, speaking frankly and seriously to his best friend.

Both boys were worried that the money Anna Matilda was paying for the girls' tutor, Miss Adele Picot, was running out. They knew she had her heart set on sending her daughters and Malley north to Philadelphia to continue their studies.

Buttie was also in Washington City traveling with his father. Neptune knew that Buttie's heart remained here on the plantation. *Why can't he be here with us, doing what he loves and comforting his Mama?* he wondered.

With a heavy heart, Neptune returned to the work of tending to the patients. He didn't like being a negative thinker and so, fighting his feelings, he tried to re-focus. His face lit up as he suddenly remembered something Lordy said to him, just before he left to study at Yale.

"You know, Neptune, I see the world as an arena. And I see myself as another George Washington or Napoleon, tho' I'm much taller and definitely more handsome. I believe I'm destined for greatness."

Neptune had punched his shoulder and ruffled his hair, leading to a friendly boxing match. If only he had him here now to provoke him into another one. Smiling at the memory, he sighed forcefully and went back to work.

Chapter Twenty

June 22, 1851

Neptune's head was spinning. There was so much to do! He and Charles were now in charge of the carriages and the horses, but Miss Anna Matilda also needed Neptune for so many other duties, and he often went for days without driving. He loved taking the family around the island in their handsome carriages, but there was little need for that these days. Georgia, Flo and Appy were attending school in Philadelphia, and Malley was studying in New Haven, Connecticut, close to Lordy. Lordy was still attending Yale University, but recently had to interrupt his studies to travel in Europe at his father's request. Buttie and Mausa Thomas King were in San Francisco, and now two of Anna Matilda's best workers were sick and lame. Neptune felt he had to be the hands and feet for his Missus, and he finally realized that it was just too much for him. He was bone tired.

Four days ago they had received a horrifying letter from Buttie in San Francisco, where he was assisting his father in his business as Customs Collector for the Port of San Francisco. Miss Anna Matilda read it aloud to the younger boys and Neptune. It had been weighing heavily on his heart since he heard it.

Buttie told them about a great fire that broke out in their hotel on May 3 at 11 p.m. Six hours later it had spread, reducing much of San Francisco to ashes. His father had just left for the country two days earlier, leaving Buttie alone to rush to the Customs House and try to save the important papers. When he returned to their hotel, he found it leveled to the ground. All their money, clothing and personal effects were burned!

The truly tragic part of Buttie's letter related that hundreds of people had lost their lives, unable to escape the fire's fury. Buttie told them he barely escaped himself. He had to descend the burning staircase of the Customs House. As he ran down the steps through the flames, he felt the scorching heat as the flames singed his back and legs.

"I just prayed and ran through it as fast as I could. I feel I've aged myself ten years in the ways and things of the world of sin and trouble. Mama, how I wished you were here to rub my head and weary body." Tears streamed down Missus Anna Matilda's cheeks as she finished his letter.

Neptune regretted poor Buttie's forced absence from the family, knowing how much he wanted to return to Retreat and work with him and Miss Anna Matilda. Yet Buttie felt a strong obligation to assist his father in his increasingly complicated career choices.

Neptune wrote to both Buttie and Lordy about his concern for their mother. Miss Anna Matilda seemed so tired and worried these days. Writing to them reminded him of a recent conversation he had with her.

"I declare, Neptune. Your mother is so fortunate to have her strong loving son with her. My boys are every which where and I can hardly remember from day to day what each one is doing. I've so little time to myself that I cannot even go to see Tootee and my grandbabies." She turned away so he would not notice tears welling up in her eyes.

"But you hab me here wif you, Missus Anna Matilda. I stay rat by yo' side lessen you axe me not to." He touched his slender fingers to her soft arm. She knew that Neptune would do anything for her, and turned to him with gratitude.

"Thank you son. But now with Mrs. Gale so crippled up and sick, I need to give her all the time I can spare." She hesitated, then added quietly, "I believe I am the greatest slave in all of Georgia. I don't have a moment to call my own."

She cannot control her nerves much longer, thought Neptune. *Miss Tootee told me that Dr. Curtis says her health is suffering, and she needs a change of scenery and climate for this nervous condition she is going through.*

Both Buttie and Lordy wrote to encourage their mother to listen to the doctor and leave the island to visit some of her children up north. She refused to heed their advice, afraid that her plantation would fail if neither she nor Thomas Butler King were living there to watch over the daily operation. Even with Overseer John Durham supervising the work, and with many loyal slaves carrying out their duties, she would not leave.

Anna Matilda's best friend Anne Fraser came to stay with her for a month. The two women consoled each other and reminisced on better times as they rocked on the front porch, drinking sweetened tea and fanning themselves against the muggy afternoon heat.

"Dear Anne, I don't think I will bear it when you move to up to Marietta. How will we see each other?" worried Anna Matilda.

"The same way we do now. We will travel to visit. After all, I come from the mainland now, and it will just be a bit further," replied Anne.

"Are you taking your people with you, or is your brother selling them off?" Anna Matilda knew that even James Hamilton Couper's resources were limited due to poor crops and other failing businesses. These were hard times for everyone in coastal Georgia.

"That's the hardest part for me. Of my twenty-one servants, I can only take seven to my new home, as we have only three cabins and just nine acres. I've asked my brother not to sell them, but to rent them out to the same plantation, if possible. He is trying to keep them together. I simply could not bear to see them separated." Anne Fraser's eyes filled with tears as Anna leaned over to comfort her.

Losing her best friend was the final heartbreak for Anna, and Neptune didn't know what to do for her. He decided to stay close to her, supporting her in every way he could. He urged the boys to speak to their father about returning for an extended stay. That would definitely lift up her spirits. And he continued to write Buttie to come back to Retreat.

Deep in his heart, Neptune felt the quickest remedy for Missus Anna Matilda's illness was to have Buttie home again. Buttie agreed, and the two of them asked Lordy to help work earnestly on a plan to bring him home.

MANHOOD

Chapter Twenty-one

June 1, 1852

"If you see my mother,
Oh yes.
Won't you tell her for me?
Oh yes.
I'm a ridin' my horse in the battlefield
I want a see my Jesus in the mornin'.
Ride on King
Ride on Conquering King,
I wanna see my Jesus in de mornin'."

They let him weep harsh sobs. They sat with him and loved him in silence. Grief filled his quiet heart. Someone had laid her body out on the bed, dressed in her Sunday best. She looked so peaceful and serene. His Missus had been "setting up" with him for hours, praying and singing with the rest of his family and friends. He finally asked her to leave them and go back to her house to get some rest.

"O Mama, I knows you be wif de Lord an' wif my sistahs now, but I cain't belief you not waitin' on me," he sobbed as he held her cold smooth hand, washing it with his steady stream of tears.

He could hear the soft and harmonious melodies they were singing behind him, but would never remember the songs that were sung. Neptune could only feel numb raw grief; his spirit was emptied out.

His father, brothers and sisters were also mourning Sukey's

death, but he couldn't speak to them now. He needed to be alone to languish in his sorrow. There would be time later to comfort his family. It seemed impossible that they were mourning yet another death.

Sukey had only been ill with the fever for several days. For the last month she and Miss Anna Matilda had been nursing his sick sisters Emiline and Mily, as well as some of the other slaves. The fever was ravaging people all over the island, and some were dying. Men and women alike were volunteering to help out in the hospitals. Both Neptune and his father spent a great deal of time coaxing Emiline and Mily to eat in spite of their raging fevers. But late one May afternoon, Emiline reached for her parents' hands, squeezed them gently, and breathed her last breath.

Sukey was devastated, but willed herself to work around the clock nursing Mily and the others in the hospital. There was no time for mourning as they watched their sixteen-year-old daughter Mily fighting her own battle with the fever. The day she finally succumbed to it, Sukey was plunged into a state of despair.

She took to her bed, wailing and refusing to eat. Grief spread over her, ripping the breath from her lungs. Neptune and his father tried everything to bring her out of it, but apathy set in. Even Linda, her fourteen-year-old child, couldn't reach her. Then Sukey too was overtaken by the scorching fever. Two days later she was gone.

"Mama, you didn't tell me go'bye," wailed Neptune. "You knows you be goin' an' you nevah eben tells me." Tortured by grief, he didn't understand that she had. She just did it in her own way.

"My son, you keep on makin' me proud." Her eyes met his as she took his hands in her small feverish ones. "I knows you an' Ila bring me granbabies and I sees dem frum my trone in Heaben."

Reminiscing on that moment, Neptune's father wiped away

his own tears with the back of his hand and watched Neptune sadly, touched by the profound pain in his boy's eyes.

I need Lordy, Neptune thought. *I miss him so much and he should be here with me. Why can't he be with me,* God? *Life is just too hard without Lordy, my sisters and now Mama. Why have You let all my loved ones go, Father? Why, why?*

Friends from Hopeton Plantation rowed Ila across the river to accompany Neptune as he sat with his mother's body through the night. She knew he needed to see her there, but he also wanted to be alone. She comforted his sisters Liddy and Linda and his brothers Abner, Sanders, and little Walter. Her young heart ached for Big Neptune, who had lost two daughters and a wife in the past month.

Sitting with his family and watching the King family's presence in the room, she thought proudly of her beloved's special position in the King household. Originally just Lordy's playmate, he had grown to become a valued member of the extended plantation family. And as she observed the special way that Neptune's brothers and father turned to him in this time of crisis, Ila knew they felt equally proud of him.

So she sat with the others, singing, moaning and praying for the family until the orange sun colored the island sky.

The following afternoon, Sukey was placed in her coffin, lined with paper cambric and covered with black calico. They carried her to the church on a one-horse wagon, which Neptune insisted on driving. The men walked single file on one side of the road and the women on the other. Reverend Andrew Neal traveled the eighty miles from Savannah, and quickly prepared the church for the funeral.

Miss Anna Matilda, perceiving the anguish and agony that Neptune was feeling because none of her older sons were with him, encouraged the other plantation owners to send as many of Sukey and Neptune's friends as they could to attend the funeral service. Several hundred slaves made their way to the church, many traveling across the river and the bay waters to be there. Neptune's father felt honored that over one hundred white friends were also in attendance.

Reverend Neal's words were kind and sincere. Everyone loved Sukey and her family. As they sang the hauntingly beautiful words to *Swing Low, Sweet Chariot,* Neptune took Ila's hand in his and walked up to the Mercy Seat in front of the pulpit. Together they knelt and prayed with his family, asking for assurance of their salvation and the peace of understanding necessary to accept these terrible losses.

As Sukey's body was driven from the church to the graveyard, the melodious notes of their hollering began in earnest.

"*Throw me any way,*
In dhat ole fiel'
Throw me any way,
In dhat ole fiel'
I don't care what you throw me
In dhat ole fiel'.
Sometimes I'm up, sometimes I'm down
In dhat ole fiel'
But still my soul is heaven boun'
In dhat ole fiel'."

The mourners continued their singing all the way to the graveyard, or "dhat ole fiel'" as they called it. Their voices resounded through the air in mixed tenor, soprano and deep bass tones. Neptune's strong baritone voice could be heard above the others as he courageously lifted his beloved mother in song to her heavenly resting place.

Chapter Twenty-two

August 28, 1853

Mausa Buttie was home! After all this time of praying him home, he really was here! Neptune danced through his daily activities singing praises to the Lord for his return. *Now if only Lordy would come back home, everything would be wonderful.*

Buttie surprised them by slipping quietly into the house during the early morning hours of August 21. Miss Anna Matilda heard footsteps in his room and cried out "Who's up there?"

"It's me, Mama!" Buttie ran down the stairs and swept her into his arms. After a tearful reunion, they scurried through the house awakening the others. Neptune, sleeping in the slave quarters, was roused from sleep by a giant bear hug and kisses on both cheeks.

"Is dat you, Mas' Buttie? My eyes ain't lyin' to me? Come let me feel yo' face an' yo' hair." After assuring himself that it was truly Buttie, Neptune turned his face away from the others to wipe away tears of happiness.

"I'm back, dearest friend. Your letters and prayers brought me home. Papa finally understood that I'm needed here with Mama and y'all, and now I'm home to stay." Buttie's joy was written all over his face. He walked through the men's quarters and woke up each of his slave friends with embraces.

Louisa and Andrew King, Thomas's brother and sister-in-law, were visiting from Cuba. They welcomed Buttie home and Louisa prepared tea. As they sat talking over steaming cups of spicy tea, Buttie related many of their travel experiences. He assured them he had left his father in good health, in spite of the outbreaks of yellow fever and cholera in New Orleans, Charleston and Savannah. Anna Matilda observed her son as he spoke, noting how thin and pale he looked. She feared he was not well.

He's under my care now, she thought, smiling to herself. *I'll get some meat on those bones. My boy is home again, thank the Lord.*

The following morning, Neptune and Buttie rode over to Hamilton Plantation to visit Tootee and William. The couple now had five children, two of whom were born during Buttie's absence. The long ride gave them an opportunity to talk about their lives.

"Mama seems pleased with the boys' education," began Buttie, referring to his younger brothers studying up north. "But she tells me young Fuddy has his tutor wrapped around his finger, and gets away with entirely too much," he laughed.

"Yes Suh, dat boy's a mess," agreed Neptune. "But Mas' Malley an' Mas' Tip bof be gittin' good marks, an' dey make yo' Mama so proud."

"How's Ila?" asked Buttie with an impish grin. "When are you two gonna marry?"

Neptune returned the grin. "She be real fine, Mas' Buttie. We see each oder bout ever month somehow. But I not be ready jet fer marriage. I save mo' money first. Doncha worry none. Ila wait fer me."

Buttie nodded and realized that he envied Neptune. Neither he nor Lordy had ever found anyone to care for in the way Neptune loved Ila. Lordy dated many women, but always expected the next one to be better. His last love, Lillie Devereaux from Savannah, had broken off the relationship because he didn't spend enough time with her. Or maybe she was bothered that he enjoyed conversing with her Uncle Eli Whitney, who had become well-known for inventing the cotton gin.

Buttie spent so much time working for his father, and so little time in one place, that he had few opportunities to get to know the young ladies he met. If only he could stay on the plantation . . .

"Neptune, you know that people in other parts of this country don't have slaves, nor do they condone slavery. I explain to them that we need slaves because of our crops, and they tell me that y'all should be freed and paid for what you do. The more I listen to that, I'm wondering if they aren't right." He paused, and asked, "Would you want to be free?"

Neptune was startled by the question, and pulled back Chaser's reins to stop. "Mas' Buttie, many ob my people axe me dat, but nevah you or Mas' Lordy. You surprise me, dat's all." He waited a few moments before continuing. "I think all men would like freedum, but I ain't shore wat I do den. If I kin stay wif yo' family an' work wif y'all, den it be good, I reckun."

"Men up north say slaves will be liberated in the next decade. They think we are cruel and wrong to own people. It's hard telling them about you and the friendship that we have, because they say we're just different from most families. Do you think we are, Neptune? Don't most people on the island treat their slaves well?"

Neptune could see that Buttie had been considering this for some time. He answered carefully, but truthfully.

"Yo' family be bettah to us den mos', Mas' Buttie. You knows dere are sum who whip dere people an' oders who keep dem on de plantations all de time. Yo' Mama eben pays us fer extra work, an' she nurses my people wen dey be sick or wif babies. So, yes, mos' people are good to dere slaves, but not like Missus Anna Matilda an' Mausa Thomas King."

They started up again and rode in comfortable silence. Neptune glanced sideways at Buttie as they rounded the bend to Hamilton. He searched his face to determine if he were upset or ill. Noticing an unfamiliar sadness in Buttie's eyes, he asked him why.

"Mas' Buttie, you be well? You be lookin' awful puny an' you ain't got no color." Neptune asked gently.

Buttie stayed quiet a long moment. Then he answered with a light shrug.

"I'm not sick with the fever, but I still have my stomach spasms and terrible headaches. Papa knows, but we haven't told Mama. When I get real tired or upset, it brings on the problems. That's probably why Papa let me come back home. He knows I love working the plantation, and just helping Mama and y'all here."

They approached the house, again lost in their own thoughts. Tootee and the children spotted them from the window, and they could hear the whoops and hollers as the little ones came tumbling down the stairs to surround them. Delighted with their welcome, both men quickly dismounted and scooped the lively children into their arms. Hoisting them onto their backs, they ran across the lawn until they collapsed, spent with laughter.

Chapter Twenty-three

January 10, 1855

What a glorious Christmas and New Year it had been! Neptune was bursting with happiness! After an absence of nearly four years, Mausa Thomas King had returned to Retreat, bringing Lordy home with him! Missus Anna Matilda seemed to forget about all her aches and pains, moving through her days with a joy her family thought she had lost forever. Neptune's constant smile lit up her heart as she watched him and Lordy sharing their news during the long separation.

As they rode across the cotton fields on their horses, they spoke to each other from the heart. Sometimes Neptune felt that they really hadn't been separated for such a long time; it seemed more like an unfolding dream.

"Mas' Lordy, yo' Mama be so much bettah wif y'all home again. Kin you see how she be wearin' her heart all ober her face?"

"Oh yes, Neptune. Now that she has Buttie working the plantation again, and you being here with her, it won't be so hard for me and Papa to go back to New York. I have to take those bar exams and give her a lawyer son." Lordy laughed nervously as he tried to imagine himself litigating the family's financial problems.

His brow furrowed in annoyance as he remembered that James Hamilton Couper was seriously considering selling Hamilton Plantation. His mother had explained that he had no choice; they were in financial ruin. They knew that Tootee and William would no longer be managing the plantation. Where would they go with five children, and another one on the way?

They rode through their world of beauty, enjoying the drenched sunlight and the shadows of the deep woods. The singing birds, the thick vines and flowing moss swaying from the green and scarlet old oaks and gum trees brought them back to the peaceful harmony of their late afternoon ride.

"Mas' Lordy, look ober yonder!" Neptune pointed to the creek beside them. "Dat's were Malley an' Jimper shot two gators last week fer Nurse Flora. She sez dat gator meat make de black chillins grow faster dan any oder food." He let out a deep-throated laugh as he turned in the saddle to study Lordy's dear face.

"Hey, Neptune, let's go alligator hunting tomorrow! We used to love to do that!" Lordy was already planning their days, and filling them with as many favorite activities as he could. It was so good to be home!

Trotting their horses through the forest they found themselves at the old town of Frederica, where the massive fort had protected their ancestors from the hostile Spanish invaders. They rode up onto the high tabby bluff and sat overlooking the river, speaking earnestly to each other about their futures.

"Soon me an' Ila gunna marry, an' I want you here fer our special day," began Neptune, his eyes glowing with copper fire. "So I tells her we wait on you to git yo' lawyah degree an' come back here to be wif us."

Lordy turned his face to search Neptune's eyes. A feeling rose up from deep inside him, like a column of wind. When it reached his mouth he found it had no voice, just a lot of longing. Bashfully, he reached across Rocket to wrap his dearest friend in a strong embrace.

"Oh, Neptune, I wouldn't miss your wedding for anything. Wherever I am, I'll come home for it. You are closer to me than even my brothers; remember, you and I are like twins." He discovered that his raw voice was quivering.

Neptune laid his hand on Lordy's arm and felt the heat flowing from his friend. How he wished Lordy could find the blessing of a woman's love! It would be awesome to share this richness of spirit with him. Yet how difficult it was to say the things that he urgently wanted to say.

"Mas' Lordy, I want fer you wat I find fer me. I axe my Lord to bring you de woman of yo' heart, even if dat takes all de room yo' heart has. Even if dere is less room fer me," he finished quietly.

Henry Lord Page King didn't know how to respond. He let out a long sigh and then looked up at the sky. Night had fallen. Breaking the spell, Neptune nudged his horse down the hill and turned around to beam at Lordy, who was following closely.

Chapter Twenty-four

March 28, 1858

"O Zion, Zion
O Zion, Zion
O Zion, Zion
When the bridegroom come.

Have oil in your vessel
When the bridegroom come,
Have oil in your vessel
When the bridegroom come,
Keep your lamp trimmed and burnin'
When the bridegroom come,
Keep your lamp trimmed and burnin'
When the bridegroom come.

We will enter into marriage,
When the bridegroom come,
We will enter into marriage,
When the bridegroom come.

O Zion, Zion
O Zion, Zion
O Zion, Zion
When the bridegroom come."

This beautiful refrain was sung as a tribute and praise to the lovely Ila, Neptune's bride. She was radiant as she entered the First African Baptist Church in her white organza gown, escorted by Neptune's best man, brother Abner. They walked down the aisle behind her two excited flower girls, who sprinkled pink and white roses in her path. Neptune had entered before her, accompanying her maid of honor and following the ushers with their lighted lamps. The guests filled the church and sang "O Zion" as the procession moved to the altar. When the ushers returned the lighted lamps to the altar, Preacher Hercules stepped forward.

"Neptune, will you take this woman to be your wedded wife?"

"Good and strong! Yes Suh!" replied Neptune, beaming his broad dimpled smile. Their friends and family cheered.

The wedding ceremony continued until Preacher Hercules offered a prayer and ended the service by asking Neptune to salute the bride.

Ila's wedding dress and shoes were selected in Savannah, Georgia. They were grateful for this generous gift from Miss Anna Matilda. Ila's plantation masters, the James Hamilton Coupers, had given them a pig to roast and many festive dishes to set their wedding table. The pound cakes and other sweets were baked by her family, and the King boys provided the wines, brandies and other spirits.

After the guests had filled themselves with the delectable feast, it was time to start the dancing. In addition to the fiddles and flutes, their friends brought along various instruments from their African heritage.

Quamina and his sons played the washboard with large thimbles. Neptune's brother Sanders blew the "quills," reed pipes made from graduated lengths of cane tightly wedged into a frame. An old ox jawbone was accompanied by a blacksmith's rasp, offering a rhythmical touch to the joyful music. Drums and heel stomping added to the percussion effect.

It should have been Neptune's perfect day, but his best friend was missing. Lordy had tried so hard to leave New Orleans where his father was working on an important political assignment. At the last minute he couldn't abandon all the work. Lordy's heart ached when he had to write Neptune the letter of explanation. Neptune wept when he received it. Brushing aside his tears, he wrote back to his dearest friend that he understood.

Little Tip was studying in New York and Fuddy was attending the University of Virginia, so they missed his wedding also. Neptune knew the King family didn't have the money to bring them home.

Buttie watched Neptune laughing with Ila, his arm lightly encircling her waist, and he ached for his lost love. For more than a year he had been seeing Miss Lettie Gamble, visiting her in Savannah whenever he could. He had believed that she was as fond of him as he was of her. Then last week, to his surprise and sorrow, she told him that she was marrying someone else. Buttie was devastated, but tried hard to mask his feelings so he wouldn't spoil Neptune's special day.

"Just think, Mama, even Neptune can marry the woman he loves, and I cannot," he whispered to Anna Matilda, sipping sweetened tea and listening to the merriment surrounding them.

"Be strong, my son. You will find your dear heart as well." Anna Matilda was concerned about her son, especially since his heartbreak seemed to have worsened his incessant heart and stomach problems.

Buttie grinned and walked over to tap Neptune on the shoulder so he could dance with the bride. Ila had been a friend of the King family since their teenage years.

"Ila, I wish you and Neptune the happiest of lives. I know Lordy would tell you the same. We are so happy for you both."

Buttie found the words of congratulations in spite of his sadness.

"Me an' Neptune be so lucky to share dis day wif you an' yo' family. Thank you for lovin' him," she answered demurely.

As Jimper drove them home in the carriage, Anna Matilda said a prayer for her husband, Lordy, Floyd and Tip: the four members of her large family who could not be there to share Neptune's happiness. As she prayed, she knew that Lordy was with them today. He was always present in Neptune's heart.

Chapter Twenty-five

March 31, 1858

Anna Matilda was beside herself with worry. Tootee, pregnant with her seventh child, was bedridden battling the whooping cough. Tootee and William's other children were also struggling to recover from it. Georgia, Appy and Flo just got over the mumps and were weak, tired and difficult. Buttie pretended to be feeling well, but Anna Matilda knew better. Then last night . . . that terrible dream had awakened her in a state of panic.

By the time she told Buttie about her dream over breakfast, she had already written about it in a letter to her husband.

"Oh Buttie, it was so realistic!" she exclaimed, dropping her fork on the china plate. "Dear Lordy was standing before me holding his right hand with his left. The right hand was covered with blood from a terrible wound, and he was pressing it to his chest, covering a gaping hole and more blood. The rain ran gently over his body, mixing with the blood and covering him with long, eerie scarlet raindrops." She shuddered as she pictured this image.

"Ah, Ma, you know that nothin' like that happens to the one we dream about," said her son to console her. "You've just had too much to worry about these past days. And Lordy will be here with us soon. That will ease your mind." He moved closer to her and gently kissed her cheek.

Anna Matilda was not comforted. Bless his heart. She knew

that Buttie was just trying to ease her fears. Yet there was so much to be anxious about. The financial situation was still straining their resources and depleting the small profits they made. There no longer seemed to be a demand for their Sea Island cotton, and the prices had fallen sharply. Other than her husband, only Neptune, her older sons and her best friend Anne knew just how bad it really was. She dared not share these problems with poor Tootee, who was so sick and now pregnant again.

What would I do if something happened to my Buttie? He is my mainstay, my rock of strength. But his heart afflictions still bring him high fevers and overall weakness. Every doctor in the area has examined him, but none can find a solution. And now Lettie left him for a wealthier man in Savannah! It's just too much for him to bear.

Lordy will be home within the month, thank God. That will bring all of us joy, especially Neptune, whose dear heart broke when Lordy couldn't be at his wedding. And he'll be able to stay with us for at least two months before returning to help Thomas.

Why can't my husband give up his dreams and political aspirations? I know he deserves success and wealth from all his hard work, but they elude him every time. His health is failing, and he cannot find proper assignments for his sons. All of this beats him down. If only he'd come home to us where he's loved and needed. We could find a way to make ends meet, the good Lord willing.

Later that evening, Neptune stepped softly into the parlor to find Miss Anna Matilda weeping as she leaned over the table, her head on her arms. He walked quietly to her and placed his hand on her heaving shoulder.

"Now, now, Missus Anna Matilda. Neptune be rat here to help you. Wat kin I do fer you?"

Lifting her head, she sniffed and wiped her cheeks with the back of her hand. Neptune could see that her nose was running as well as her eyes. She turned to him and poured out her pain.

"Neptune, I know you understand love," she began. "It's the strongest force in the world, and when it's blocked, then comes pain." Her voice cracked as she wiped again at her eyes and nose.

"I was just asking the Lord to open up another route for that love to travel. I keep trying to push it through my heart to where I think it should go, but it's not for me to decide its path." She studied his eyes. "Do you understand what I'm trying to say?" She shrugged, her hands falling loosely in her lap.

Neptune kneeled in front of her and picked up each of her tired hands. "Yes, M'am, I do. I always knows wat's in yo' heart. You be one wunderful lady, and I be so lucky to hab you fer my Missus." He kissed her cold fingers and rubbed them between his warm palms.

Slowly Anna Matilda stood up, and found she was smiling at him as warmth and strength returned to her body. This dear man could always do this for her. His unconditional love was one of her greatest blessings. Pulling him off his knees, she linked her arm through his to lead him across the room, just as thunder rumbled over the skies.

"Neptune, let's make a fire. We must talk about another important matter."

Neptune built the fire as she gathered her thoughts. When he sat down at her side, she studied his face for a long moment.

"Neptune, it pains my heart that although you and Ila are married, she is living in Hopeton and you are here with us. I'm going to speak to James Hamilton Couper about purchasing her and bringing her here to live with you."

Neptune rose to his feet, flushed from happiness. "Ay, Missus Anna Ma . . ."

"Sit down, son. Don't thank me yet. We still have the money matter to work out. I know Miss Ila is a valuable servant at Hopeton Plantation, but since she belongs to my best friend

Anne's brother, I trust we'll be able to agree on her price."

Neptune knew full well how difficult the financial situation was. He also knew that when his Missus set her mind to something, she would achieve it.

He moved his chair closer to her and took her hands in his. "Thank you, Missus Anna Matilda. You talk to me bout findin' anuder route fer yo' love to travel. Den you tell me you worried bout me an' Ila bein' separated. You already find a new road to send yo' love. You send it back to us, an' we be grateful to you forevah."

She stood up to embrace him, and held him for a long time before pulling away with a smile on her worn face.

Looking up into his luminous eyes, she declared, "Neptune, it's time to get some work done!"

Neptune beamed. He knew his Missus was going to be fine.

Chapter Twenty-six

January 30, 1859

The inhabitants of Retreat Plantation were enveloped in sorrow. It did not seem possible that they could withstand another tragedy, yet Christmas of 1858 had been so solemn that it passed almost undetected. Rhina's daughter Annie died of fever in early October, at the tender age of fourteen. She was a favorite of Anna Matilda, and both Rhina and Anna were inconsolable. Thomas Butler King experienced bad health and sickness throughout the fall and winter and remained in Louisiana, so his wife could not even take care of him. Tootee, thin and weak and heavy with her seventh child, was plagued with constant attacks of palpitation of the heart. She could hardly eat and when she did, she lost it all. Yet she remained patient and cheerful throughout her suffering.

On November 4, 1858, Tootee's tiny baby, Thomas Butler Couper, was born, healthy but weak. Two hours later Tootee almost lost her life. The family and slaves rallied around her, begging the Lord to spare her, and He did. Neptune, Lordy and Buttie were there to give Anna Matilda the support she so badly needed. Right before Christmas Buttie and Malley left to discuss possible business connections for the King family, so Lordy was the only son home for Christmas. He and Neptune did their best to brighten up the holidays, at least for the grandbabies.

In early January Anna Matilda and Buttie traveled to Savannah to purchase a tract of land in Lounds County. Anna Matilda left him there and returned to her plantation, awaiting the arrival of her husband. By January 16, Lordy, Buttie and their father had all returned home. Even without Floyd and Tip, who were still studying up north, these few days were some of the happiest the King family had shared in years.

Three days after the arrival of Lordy and their father, Buttie experienced acute heart pain and stayed in bed until late afternoon. He got up to eat supper with his family and then took a walk with his father and sisters. The next day they all rode over to say goodbye to Tootee and William, before they left for Savannah. The boys and Thomas Butler King rode horseback, while the women went by carriage. After returning to Retreat they drank their afternoon hot tea, which seemed to give Buttie an attack of the hiccups. Neptune later told everyone that Buttie still had the hiccups when he went to sleep that night.

The following morning during his breakfast preparation, Buttie noticed his face was swollen. He went to the table to show his family and discovered he had trouble articulating distinctly. Thomas Butler King took hold of his hand to lead him to his room, and felt it stiffen and spasm.

"Oh Papa, I feel the spasm extending all over me," he managed to get out between gasping breaths. "I think this is the end." Buttie was ashen and trembling as Neptune stripped him and placed his feet into a hot tub.

His mother rubbed his swollen chest with painkiller, forcing herself to hold back her sobs. Neptune galloped Chaser down to the pier to dispatch a boat to fetch Dr. Curtis. Anna Matilda drew a hot bath for Buttie. Then they wrapped him in blankets and placed him in his bed.

"I feel like sleep, Mama. Please put wet towels on my head. The palpitations are back and are making me nauseous. Please

Malley, put your finger down my throat. I can't do it myself because my hands won't function."

Malley obeyed him. Buttie vomited up his food and a great deal of blood. His family was frightened and horrified, praying that it was from a ruptured blood vessel, and not from the heart.

Buttie rested for an hour, while Thomas Butler King and Neptune went outside to see if the boat had returned yet with Dr. Curtis. Walking back from the dock to the house, they heard Anna Matilda's bloodcurdling scream.

Racing up the wooden steps and into the house, they found Malley and Lordy holding Buttie down on the bed while their mother elevated his head with her strong hands. His sisters watched in fear as his body, wracked with convulsions, jerked uncontrollably. Buttie's eyes were opened wide, yet he seemed oblivious to those around him. As Thomas Butler King attempted to take blood from his arm, Buttie's body pitched upward, and then fell back on the bed in complete relaxation. He took three breaths, quiet as an infant, and went limp.

"No, no dear God," moaned his mother, "his noble soul is leaving his body. I can feel it lifting." She slumped over in her chair, holding his hand to her breast. "My baby, my precious Buttie," she sobbed harshly.

Buttie had been gone only fifteen minutes when Dr. Curtis rushed through the doorway. The doctor gently assured the family that they could not have done any more for him. It was likely that he had a congenital heart defect or a cardiac injury from a childhood illness, such as rheumatic fever. He had suffered an embolic stroke and thrown up a blood clot from the damaged part of his heart. That would account for the paralysis of his face and extremities. Dr. Curtis believed that Buttie died from internal bleeding, perhaps the result of gastritis or an ulcer caused by the extreme stress of his terminal illness.

Neptune knelt by the bed and picked up his other hand. Tears began filling his eyes and he wept with a bowed head and a heart gouged with pain.

"Buttie, you always be so lovin', so cheerful, so good to us all. Yo' soul be wif God an' yo' Savior now." Finally, Neptune stood up and held out Buttie's hand for Lordy as he retreated to the back of the room. Walking by the girls, huddled and frightened in the corner, he hugged them to his heart. "We mus' let him go wif' peace," he told them quietly. Appy sobbed into his shoulder, her small body shaking in disbelief.

Anna Matilda and her husband huddled together as he held her up at the edge of the bed. "Oh God, give us the strength to bear up under this terrible affliction," he pleaded. Wailing loudly, Anna Matilda sank to the floor, pulling Thomas with her. "It's too much for us to endure. The weight of my grief is crushing me."

Georgia and Flo fell weeping to the floor next to their mother, racked with terrible pain. As the afternoon shadows faded into night, Neptune and the family mourned Buttie, connected by a cord of grief and devastation.

Chapter Twenty-seven

August 23, 1859

Anna Matilda could not cope with Buttie's death, even for her family's sake. So much had been ripped from her soul; she felt tortured by grief and anguish so intense it scraped her nerves raw. One evening Neptune found her sitting alone in her favorite garden, weeping inconsolably. Her sad face glimmered with moon-bright tears. Wrapping her in his arms for comfort, he realized how limp and thin the once strong, robust Anna Matilda had become, a skeleton of her former self.

"Talk to me, Missus Anna Matilda. Tell yo' Neptune yo' troubles. He listen all you need." He spoke softly as she rocked in his arms.

"Oh, Neptune, I just want to lie down in this garden and stay here for the rest of my life," she murmured, trying to sit up. "Missing my Buttie takes every waking minute, all my energy and time. I am so thirsty for him. I just want to go be with him in peace with our Lord."

"Missus, doncha talk like dat. Yo' family an' friends needs you wif us. You be de light we follow."

"No, Neptune, not any longer. My light is gone and my heart is tired. Buttie's death has emptied my spirit." She began rocking again, tears streaming as she cried. Neptune held her quietly.

Two months earlier, just after Buttie's passing and just before Lordy and Thomas Butler King had to reluctantly leave Retreat, Lordy told his parents he wanted to speak to them about an important issue. Because it was so serious, he even practiced his presentation with Neptune before meeting with them. They agreed to listen to what he had to say after supper that evening.

"Mama and Papa, I know there is no good time to discuss finances and new proposals, but what I want to tell you is something that Buttie believed in and shared with Neptune and me before his death. I don't think he ever had the opportunity to speak to you about it."

Anna Matilda sat up straight at the mention of Buttie's name. Her tired yet alert eyes silently questioned him.

"Buttie and I always respected and obeyed your wishes, even as boys when we were willful and wanted our way. We learned that you usually proved to be right. But the issue of slavery has bothered both of us since we went away to study in the north, where they are vehemently opposed to it." He paused, searching his parents' faces for clues to their response.

"We've asked Neptune and some of our other people about this issue, and they all feel that slavery is wrong. Don't misunderstand me, please. None of our people say they are unhappy with their circumstances here at Retreat, but that may be out of loyalty to you. Can you honestly believe that anyone wants to be owned by another?"

"Lordy, what exactly did Neptune tell you when you asked him?" Anna Matilda asked anxiously.

"He told us not to worry about him, because he is already free in Christ and no one can take that away. He told us we can only own his body," answered Lordy honestly.

"What on earth are you proposing, Son? That we free all our people and shut down our plantations?" asked Thomas, upset by his son's words.

"No, Sir. Buttie, Neptune and I talked about what will happen when slavery is eventually abolished, which many believe will happen. The cotton and rice crops will be replaced by industry and timber growing or who knows what. Our professors told us that there is going to be a tremendous demand for timber for railroads and ships. We have huge amounts of timber on our lands!

"Like you, Papa, we could be visionaries here at Retreat and begin by freeing our people and then hiring them to work in our new business. That way, they wouldn't have to wander up north looking for work, and we would gain by having loyal and intelligent people starting this venture with us." Lordy felt drained and paused to collect his thoughts.

Anna Matilda spoke with thoughtful determination.

"Lordy, my father created this plantation and taught me exactly how to run it. It has worked all these years and given all of us what we've needed. This could only have been done through slave labor, and our people have also benefited from the system. I've worked so hard to pass this legacy on to you and your siblings. And I'm just too weary to do anything else."

"Oh, Mama," Lordy said, "but now Sea Island cotton is no longer prosperous and the fields are tired. We need to do something else with our land—and quickly. If our people will be freed anyway, why not be the first to free them and let them stay on with us as paid workers?" Lordy was excited that they were even considering his option.

"Lordy," replied Thomas, "you have seen where my visionary schemes have ended. Most of them have lost us money and reputation. I'm through with taking big risks. If it comes down to abolishing slavery, we'll comply and hope our people want to stay with us for wages. But don't ask me to initiate it on this island, because that won't happen," said Thomas.

Lordy wanted to make sure that his parents knew that Neptune would not let them down.

"But Neptune would convince all the others to stay with us, help start a new business and teach them how to care for their families, like you've always done for us, Papa."

Anna Matilda stood slowly and put her arms around his waist. "You've always done well by following your heart, Lordy. If what you describe comes to be one day, I'm certain you'll make it work."

Lordy followed them out of the room, relieved that he had shared one of his and Buttie's most important concerns.

A week later, he and his father left the plantation for business dealings.

The remaining family members continued to visit Buttie's room, speaking of him often and mingling their tears. For a brief time, their company provided Anna Matilda with a measure of solace, but gradually she weakened and wanted to grieve alone.

She re-read Buttie's letters describing how grateful he was to have such a perfect family. In a letter to her husband she wrote how much Buttie had loved them on earth, and how he must love them even more in his new and far happier home in Heaven.

"Dearly beloved, I saw Buttie in the mirror of my soul," she wrote. She told him that she would pray that death would bring her a reunion with their departed treasures.

Anna Matilda became even more spiritual and trusting of her Heavenly Father as time elapsed. On May 5, 1859, after urgent letters from Neptune, both Lordy and Thomas returned to the island; three days later Tip arrived. Although Anna's family was slowly re-uniting, her mind remained far away.

In July, they received the disturbing news that Thomas Butler King had not been re-nominated for his U.S. Congressional seat. For the first time ever, Anna Matilda did not react to this news. Yet despite her state of apathy, she told them she felt the presence of God looking down on her. She continued to communicate with Buttie in the room where he died.

"Precious Buttie, I've been dumped in the ocean during a terrible storm. I'm tossed by the water and thrashed against the rocks. I fight daily to keep afloat. Part of me doesn't even want to keep my head above water. If I only knew I would be with you, I would stop fighting and just sink away."

Perhaps she received an answer. Seven months after Buttie's death, with her family nearby, Anna Matilda died of a broken heart. She simply gave up the will to live and allowed herself to sink away from shore. Her husband found her lying peacefully on her canopied bed with Buttie's letters spread across her breast.

Chapter Twenty-Eight

August 22, 1860

Neptune and Ila bowed their heads at Anna's graveside. Today was the first anniversary of her death, and the floral arrangement they brought her was the finest one Ila had ever made, using Anna's favorite flowers from her gardens. Yet it seemed dwarfed by all the others placed by her stone by the islanders, black and white. They all loved her enormously.

Neptune and Ila's one-year-old daughter Leanora came with them and sat on the stone next to Anna Matilda's grave. She prattled cheerfully to Buttie's spirit with soft, sweet, unintelligible words. Lordy often took her with him when he visited his mother and brothers, so she felt comfortable playing there in the graveyard. Neptune and Ila knew they had been blessed that Leanora was born three months before Anna Matilda died, and that she had held her and loved her like her own grandbaby. Sometimes they felt their Missus's presence within their daughter's heart.

Since Anna Matilda's death, the King family's home life was beginning to unravel. Mausa Thomas Butler King left Lordy and Malley in charge of the plantation and drowned his grief in a whirlpool of political activities. He had not been in favor of the southern state's secession from the rest of the American Union. Neptune understood this ongoing dilemma more clearly after speaking to Lordy.

"Neptune, terrible things are happening to our country. The

northern states are angry over the issues of slavery and states' rights, like tariffs and the expansion of slavery. Our Governor Brown is now in agreement with the Unionist views. Papa agrees with him on giving each state its rights, but opposes the idea of our state seceding from the Union. Do you understand all of this?" asked Lordy, squinting his eyes in the mid-day sun.

"Yes, Mas' Lordy, I think so. You sez dat states be arguin' ober to hab slaves an' wat should dey do bout dere laws." Neptune had been listening closely to these political discussions for some time now.

"But Papa told me that when the voting comes in, he will have to follow the southern cause and support his governor," added Lordy, with concern. "That's what confuses me. I'm sure that will mean even more trips away from home for him. I don't like the fact that he's already traveling so much between Washington City and our capital at Milledgeville.

"Papa tells us that at the Democratic Convention last April, the new Republican Party nominated Abraham Lincoln. He advocates an end to the expansion of slavery, and most southerners don't follow his platform."

"Mas' Lordy, wat happin' if dis man Abram Linkun win? Wat happin' to us slaves? Kin we still live wif y'all?" This was the part of the discussion that most concerned him and the other black people at Retreat.

"Don't worry, Neptune. You'll always have a place with us. The major concern of the Unionists is that slavery doesn't advance to more states. And that we don't bring any more people over from Africa. You know that hasn't happened for a time now."

Neptune and Lordy were united on this political issue as well as on the other ones. They both believed that Thomas Butler King knew enough about what was good for their state for them to support and follow his political beliefs. They talked about how difficult it was for Lordy's father to stay on Retreat Plantation with his wife no longer there. Malley was capable of managing Retreat with the help of his slaves, and Lordy would have to leave soon. He had just been admitted to the bar in New York, and would finally practice law in the state he had chosen.

As Neptune and his family were leaving the cemetery, they met Georgia, Flo and Appy, carrying large bouquets of flowers from the gardens to their mother's grave. Neptune thought about his Missus and how pleased she would be with all the adoration she received from her loved ones. *I jes knows dat she sees us frum up dere in Heaben, sittin' side by side wif Mas' Buttie. I kin feel it in my bones.* Holding Leanora's tiny hand with his large one, he led them up the path back to the house.

Chapter Twenty-Nine

June 13, 1861

Abraham Lincoln's election as U.S. President was the last straw for some southern states that were already thinking about seceding from the Union. On December 20, 1860, South Carolina became the first southern state to secede, followed rapidly by Mississippi, Florida and Alabama. The Confederate States of America were created.

On January 19, 1861, when Georgia became the fifth state to secede from the Union, the people of St. Simons Island did not yet understand that their lives were about to change forever. Although many of them did not support secession, they were willing to wait patiently for guidance, depending heavily on Thomas Butler King for instructions. On April 12, 1861, a Confederate cannon opened fire on a small U.S. Federal garrison at Fort Sumpter, near Charleston, South Carolina. That act plunged the nation into the Civil War, later dubbed by northerners and southerners alike as "that great blast of ruin and destruction."

Thomas King's sons, like many of the young men in the area, were excited about joining in the fight against the Union. But they knew that leaving might put their plantations at risk. Georgia was an agricultural state that depended on the railroads and steamboats to carry their products to market. It lacked the population, capital and experience in manufacturing and industry to successfully wage war, but its citizens were willing to do what they could.

Governor Joseph E. Brown instructed Thomas Butler King to prepare for a mission to England, France and Belgium to strengthen shipping ties between Georgia and those countries. Knowing that the northern blockade of southern ports would soon limit key exports, Thomas sent an urgent request to Governor Brown and the Confederate President Jefferson Davis to immediately ship all the available cotton abroad. This would build up the Confederate treasury and protect the interest of all plantation owners. Sadly, the Governor did not follow this advice and the cotton piled up in the warehouses. By the time the blockade closed the ports, credit had shrunk and the plantation owners were ruined.

President Lincoln's call for troops brought jeers from the southern press. Who would volunteer to go out to fight and how would they be paid? But their predictions would be proven wrong. Southerners thought that the justice and invincibility of their cause would prevail. Enlisted Confederate soldiers looked forward almost gaily to the upcoming conflict, their optimism fueled by promises of military assistance from their leaders, as well as by their glorious principle of patriotism.

All four King brothers enlisted in June of 1861, along with their eligible friends and neighbors. As soon as Neptune heard about it, he went looking for Lordy.

"Mas' Lordy, wen you be goin' to de war, I be goin' wif you. You needs me to cook yo' favorite foods an' help you wif de heavy guns."

Lordy was astonished. His head snapped around and he stared at his lifelong friend. "Neptune, you have a wife and a daughter. Soon you'll have another baby. Your place is here with your family, protecting them and my sisters from the enemy."

"No Suh, my place be nexta you." Neptune stood tall, his chocolate eyes locked on Lordy's. "Dat be de promise I make to yo' Mama wen we talk in de garden. My Ila knows dis is wat I hafta do."

Lordy was deeply moved by Neptune's loyalty. Knowing that he and his brothers would most likely be assigned to different regiments, he was selfishly pleased to have Neptune by his side. But he would never want to put him in harm's way.

Rules had already been devised governing the presence of slaves. They could assist their masters as personal servants, but they could not fire a shot in battle. Some of the wealthier men would take more than one slave. Lordy's brothers had decided not to take anyone, leaving as many strong men as possible on the plantation to do the work. Neptune insisted on joining Lordy in military service and eventually wore him down. Once Lordy agreed to it, they began their preparations.

Meanwhile, Governor Brown followed orders from General Robert E. Lee and sent down 1,500 state troops to offset the naval blockade that he knew the North was planning for Brunswick's deep harbor. These troops, with the help of slave labor, built a strong fort on the south end of St. Simons Island that would protect the St. Simons Sound approach to Brunswick.

With the arrival of the troops, the decision was made to store much of the battle equipment on the Retreat property. Soon a garrison of soldiers moved in. The King girls wasted no time befriending the soldiers, and Retreat Plantation once again buzzed with music and laughter. Everyone felt certain that the war would be won by the Confederate soldiers in no time at all.

One frequent visitor to Retreat Plantation was young and beautiful Eugenia Grant from the Elizafield Plantation near Brunswick. She and Malley had known each other from childhood. They spent many happy hours together, frequently dancing in the elegant dining room lit by silver candles. They flirted on long moonlit horseback rides and walks on the beach. Lordy observed this attraction with amusement; preoccupied as he was with his imminent departure.

His sister Georgia was also receiving attention, and Lordy wasn't the only one to notice.

"Mas' Lordy, hab you seen Miss Georgia makin' dem eyes at Colonel William? She sing to him an' blush wen he takes her hand." Neptune wanted to be sure that Lordy was aware of this other romance unfolding on the plantation.

"I'll have a word with her about this. He's here to command the troops, not to pursue my sister," answered Lordy, yanking the saddle off Rocket and heaving it to the floor.

When he later spoke to Georgia, she confided to him that she was falling in love. With her father away on his mission in Europe, Georgia poured out her frustrations and confusion to her older brother.

"Ay, Lordy, it's such a tangled mess. Please hear me out, and be gentle with me," she added, noticing his deeply furrowed brow. "Dear William is a widower, but a Roman Catholic. His church believes in only one marriage. But we want to be together. Can you think of a way to help us out?"

Lordy was shocked at the intensity of her feelings and told her so. Nevertheless, after speaking to the Colonel, he decided to sanction their plans and give them his blessings.

"Georgia, I'm sure this is what Mama would have wanted for you." Lordy smiled fondly at his little sister and hugged her close to him, choking back tears.

The Episcopal Church in Brunswick agreed to marry them, and by summer's end little Georgia had become Mrs. William Duncan Smith.

During William's short leave from duty, the couple honeymooned at the Pulaski House in Savannah. Oddly enough, when Flo insisted on accompanying them, the bride and groom allowed it.

"Dat sho' be strange, doncha think, Mas' Lordy? I wundah wat de Colonel think bout de sistahs?" laughed Neptune, shaking his head.

"Well, you know how Flo can't bear to be separated from her adored Georgia? At least she had her own room." Lordy joined him in the merriment, slapping him affectionately on the shoulder as they headed back up to the house.

Chapter Thirty

July 30, 1861

Soft melodies echoed off the bay as the black men made music and talked in the moonlight. Once a month they gathered together at one of the plantations to sing and talk. Tonight they were down by the dock at Retreat.

Neptune and Adam tried to make sense of the current news as they sat around the campfire.

"Yo' Mausa not happy wif dis secession, right Adam?" asked Neptune, pleased that he could spend the evening with his friend from Kelvin Grove Plantation.

"No, he be a Unionist like yo' Mausa King. Wat you think gunna happin' wif us?" Adam was not as educated as Neptune and valued his friend's opinion.

"I dunno, Adam. Summa us might could go to war wif our Mausas if dey go. Mausa Lordy tells me dat his papa sez de folks up north gunna cum to de south an' fight. He talks to de Govner Brown so dey knows things we don't know jet."

Jimper and Sam moved up from the water and settled in closer to the fire. A few of the slaves were still making music, but most of them had drawn closer to the fire to take part in the conversation.

"I wanna go up an' help our people fight agains' dem Yankees." Sam spoke with passion as he sipped from his bottle.

"Doncha know dat dem Yankees want fer us slaves to be free?"

countered Nathaniel, who had come down from Westpoint Plantation for their reunion. "Dey wanna help us so why we gunna fight 'em?"

Neptune, listening closely to this discussion among his friends, wasn't sure how he felt about it. After President Lincoln's election as U.S. President, the southern states began to leave the Union one by one. The President believed that slavery was wrong, and the northern people agreed. President Lincoln knew the agricultural states needed slaves to work the lands, but wanted to set them free and have them receive payment to work just like white people. Was this possible?

"Will y'all wanna be leavin' yo' white families to git yo' own cabins? Den you work fer yo' food an' make yo' clothes. Ain't no Missus gunna sew fer you," said Jimper.

"But we be free! We do wat we want an' nobody owns us no mo'!" Nathaniel couldn't believe his friends were not excited about this opportunity for freedom.

The debate continued as the black men fed the fire and drank moonshine from an earthen jug. Neptune noticed that none of them sounded convinced one way or the other. Most of them wanted yet feared the idea of freedom. No one knew what to expect from it, and they were generally content with their lives now. Freedom would mean separation from all they knew. It meant independence, and fending for themselves.

"Yes Suhs, but nobody own us no mo' if we be free!" exclaimed Adam enthusiastically. "We knows how to work hard an' we gits paid to do it wen we be free."

The night turned to silence as they digested this. Finally, Neptune spoke.

"I go wif my Mausas King wen dey go to fight. Wen it be ober, den we know wat we gunna do."

"Neptune, you got a bettah life den mos' slaves. Yo' white family treat you real good an' give you everthing you want. But think of de res' of us. Nobody wants to b'long to nobody," reasoned Adam, sadness creeping through his words.

"We all got good white families here. I stays wif my family. If dey wanna me to help 'em, I do dat," added Sam.

"Not me. I git my chance to go up north, I be gone. I think Prezden' Linkun be right. All men needa be free an' own demselfs!" Nathaniel spoke forcefully, looking around the group for affirmation. Many of them shook their heads in agreement.

It was getting late and there was plenty to think about. Alone or in pairs, the men said their farewells and began the walk back to their plantations. A few rode out on horseback. When they had all left, Neptune turned to walk up the stone path to his cabin, wondering how Ila would react when he recounted this conversation.

As his hand rested on the rough gate latch he suddenly smiled. Life was so good with Ila by his side. She was such a blessing, along with Leanora and the new baby to come! He knew they could weather any storm together.

Chapter Thirty-one

August 10, 1861

The moment he'd been dreading had come. They sat in the small room where they ate and relaxed. Leanora was asleep in the far corner. A light summer breeze drifted through their single small window set deep into the tabby wall.

Neptune noticed that Ila was wearing his favorite smock, the simple blue muslin one covered with tiny flowers. It wasn't made to serve as a maternity dress, yet she looked heartbreakingly beautiful in it.

Neptune held her close, comforting her and wiping the tears sliding down her cheeks. His heart ached as he felt her body, extended with their baby, shaking with sobs. He begged her to listen to him.

"Ila, love, hush yoself now. Think about our lil' baby you be rockin' wif yo' sobs," he murmured softly.

"I be thinkin' bout that chile ain't gunna hab a Papa wen he be born," retorted Ila, hurt and angry.

"Course he gunna hab his Papa. He jes be away fer a spell." Neptune spoke calmly and tenderly, feeling her body begin to relax. She reached out to their simple table to thoughtfully finger the tiny carved rocking horse he had made for the baby.

For the past hour and a half, Neptune had tried to explain to Ila why he must go to the war with Lordy and his brothers. She made him explain over and over why men had to settle their problems by fighting.

"Cain't dey jes talk an' find a ways to agree? By fightin', nobody evah wins, an' everone loses," she countered, exasperated.

"Ila, de country be divided in dere demands. De states break up now an' de country gotta be fixed." Neptune remembered conversations with the King boys when they were certain that keeping the Union together was the best thing for the country.

"Prezden' Linkun sez 'A house divided agains' itself cain't stand.'"

He had put off telling her until he knew the time was drawing near to leave. Now the King boys were preparing their departure and he needed to make her understand why he had to accompany them. His own burlap sack, sitting inside the front door, seemed to reproach him.

"Neptune, you be married wif one chile an' anoder almos' here. Nobody sez you gotta go north! Yo' place be here wif us!" Ila sputtered out the words between heaving breaths.

Neptune sat down on the floor in front of her to take her hands in his. As he massaged them, he breathed in the sweet familiar smell of her skin. He rubbed them, slowly and leisurely, one at a time, trying to help her body relax.

"My sweet baby, you be mo' important to me den anybody. Even Mausa Lordy, an' yo know how I loves him. But I make a promise to his Mama jes before she dies, out dere in her favorite garden. I promise to always watch out fer him an' protek him howevah I kin."

Ila nodded slightly against his chest and Neptune lifted her chin with two fingers and smiled into her still stormy eyes.

"Ila, I also told Lordy wen we was jes kids dat I will always bring him home. You remembahs dat story he told you, doncha?"

Ila's hand flexed briefly as though she were about to jerk it away. Slowly her fingers closed over his and squeezed hard, clinging, begging for mercy.

"Yes Suh, I knows you made bof dem promises. I knows you be a man of yo' word. Dats de man I love. Go, Neptune, go an' help dose boys. We be fine here, an' de good Lord bring you back to me so you sees yo' new son." Ila stood up, strong and proud, and folded herself into Neptune's embrace.

Neptune shut his eyes to hold back tears of his own. He felt peaceful about his decision, knowing it was what he must do. *"Oh Father, wrap your arms around my babies and my woman,"* he prayed. *"I know you will be with me, and I beg you to bless their days and keep them safe. Amen."*

Chapter Thirty-two

January 10, 1862

The train carrying Lordy and Neptune to Camp Georgia pulled into Richmond's ornate railroad station early one afternoon. A soldier in a smart gray uniform appeared from the crowd on the platform and introduced himself as Sergeant Hollis. He said that Captain Francis Ward had instructed him to drive Lt. King and his manservant to the Camp in the company's buggy.

"Thank you, Sergeant," Lordy said. "And perhaps you can explain why a Camp for troops from Georgia has been located so far north, in Virginia."

"Good question, Sir," the thickset soldier answered while loading Lordy's bags into the back of the buggy. "Being closer to the battleground means faster deployment, and makes it easier for soldiers to catch up with their fast-moving regiments. Located here, the Camp also provides added protection against any Yankee incursions."

Thirty minutes later Lordy could feel the excitement building inside him as they pulled into the Camp. Hundreds of young soldiers were half hidden by smoke lifting weakly from a dozen smoldering campfires. One small phalanx of men was marching under the watchful eyes of an officer. Others busily cleaned long rifles in front of the quartermaster's tent, talking and smoking pipes, or watching two older men start a new fire with a "fireball" fashioned of coal dust, sawdust, sand and wet clay.

Neptune and Lordy had never seen such a variety of busy men in one place. Young boys carrying musical instruments bumped shoulders with unshaven farmers in overalls, and a serious discussion held beside a stack of wooden crates might have been taking place in front of a courthouse.

"Mas' Lordy, dis place is much biggah den I eben imagines. Do you think Mas' Malley, Mas' Fuddy an' Mas' Tip gunna be in sum place lik dis one?" asked Neptune, eyes wide with amazement.

Inside the command tent Captain Ward noted Lordy's arrival in a large logbook before introducing him to Rushen Rose, another young lieutenant who had evidently just arrived the day before. Lieutenant Rose was a thin man with a surprisingly big belly. Across his narrow chin was a sparse, strawberry-blond beard, and his dark green eyes wore a permanent glare. But he invited Lordy to stop by the tent he shared with two other officers after getting settled in.

Captain Ward detailed a passing private to help Lordy and Neptune carry their cases. After quickly unpacking they walked across a corner of the parade ground to find Lieutenant Rose.

Lordy entered Rose's tent to pay his respects. Neptune approached an older black man, sitting on an overturned wooden pail beside the tent and idly whittling on a stick. Neptune was eager to make his acquaintance, but couldn't help noticing the narrow cluster of thin scars that seemed to wrap around the slave's neck like a noose.

Just then, from inside the tent came an unpleasant shouted command.

"Tigerhead, finish polishing my boots!"

"Yassuh, Mausa Rushen," the slave drawled back. "Dey be done rat away."

Then to Neptune's astonishment, Tigerhead reached behind

him to pick up a riding boot from the dirt, brush it quickly with his sleeve, and toss it back over his shoulder.

Neptune had never seen a slave act like this. He wondered what could make slave and master treat each other this way and decided to introduce himself and try to find out.

"Hello, friend, my name is Neptune from S'n Simons Islan'. Dis be our first day here in camp. Is everting all right wif you?"

Tigerhead's eyes narrowed with some grim memory and he turned his back to the tent before answering in the murmur reserved for conversations between slaves.

"You see dese marks," he said, touching his neck. "Overseer Mr. Sturgis thinks I be too uppidy one day an' he cum to my room wif a cat-o-nine-tails hangin' over his shoulder. He wrap dem beaded strings round my neck and he pull, three times. Den I gets back on my feet, lookin' him straight bak in de eyes an' holdin' de ends of dat cat. He nevah beat me since den, so I guess you kin say yes Suh, everting's all right wif me."

Just then Neptune heard the unfamiliar sound of Lordy's raised but controlled voice in anger, similar to the fury Neptune was feeling.

"Now we must go prepare to bed down, Lieutenant Rose," Lordy was saying over his shoulder in a strained voice. "You will excuse us, I trust."

A confused-looking Lieutenant Rose peered out of the tent and over Lordy's shoulder toward Neptune.

"Oh, is there someone else in your party?" he asked.

Lordy, pausing next to his friend looked back and said quietly,"Yes Sir, and Neptune is all the company I need tonight."

Back at Lordy's tent they began setting up an oiled burlap lean-to, under which Neptune could rest when he didn't want to return to the tent set up for slaves.

Neptune, sensing that Lordy would be thinking about Retreat, asked in a conversational tone, "Mas' Lordy, wat you think yo' dear Mama might say about dis place?"

Straightening up with a cypress stake in his hand, Lordy answered, "I suspect she would be surprised and a mite disappointed."

"Yes Suh," Neptune concurred. "She might wondah why you be fightin' to hep out deses people you ain't nevah gunna be invitin' to Retreat."

Like the Coupers and other Unionist planters, the Kings had just recently set aside their anti-secession stance at the request of Governor Brown.

"Mebbe she say," Neptune continued, "that if we be fightin' fer sumting we believe in, it be fer the good."

Lordy found himself touched at yet another perceptive comment from Neptune. "That's right, Neptune," he replied. "And she always taught us that treating others with respect just makes good sense, but it is also an act of living faith. With enough faith we help each other grow and prosper."

For a long moment Neptune busied himself straightening some personal effects in a small wooden chest he had placed at the foot of his lean-to.

"An' wile we be helpin' folks we dunna care fer, woud she expek us to try an' help people like dat Lieutenan'?" he wondered aloud.

"There's probably not much we can do, my friend," Lordy replied, "except to refuse to live like those people who hurt others."

Chapter Thirty-three

February 26, 1862

At the outset of the war, Thomas Butler King was convinced that St. Simons Island would be attacked and he sent word to his family and slaves to evacuate. During the final days of 1861 they moved to an inland plantation in Ware County that he had acquired for such a purpose. In a letter to his daughters, he specified slaves who should build rafts to transport stock and farm implements, crop seed, food supplies, furniture, slaves and other valuables. While they were preparing final details, a message came to the inhabitants of St. Simons Island from General Robert E. Lee. Attempting to organize the defense of Georgia from his base in Savannah, he realized that he could no longer protect them from the Union Navy. He asked them to leave quickly and move inland.

By late February of 1862, General Lee realized that Union forces were overtaking them, and decided to evacuate his military forces as well. Wanting to leave no military aids for the enemy regiments, before decamping they blew up the recently built fort and the lighthouse. Less than a month later, the Union forces formally occupied St. Simons Island.

The King family left most of their valuables behind in the rush to evacuate. That same night a heavy storm sank most of the rafts, but no lives were lost.

With the King sons all away at battle, Thomas King asked William Audley Couper to protect and care for the women, children and slaves. Georgia's husband was also away fighting, and once again the sisters were living together with their slaves.

A short time later in March of 1862, a Federal Naval force headed by Samuel DuPont occupied St. Simons Island. They immediately liberated all the plantation slaves and made the island their base for naval raids on Georgia's towns and plantations. Some moved into Retreat Plantation, rounding up the "contraband Negroes" from the other plantations and housing them there. These slaves were put to work planting cotton and corn, and were given rations and clothing. The officers also collected booty and many valuable possessions from Retreat and other plantation houses.

It was a blessing that Thomas Butler King, his children, his slaves, and the other island residents were not yet aware of the plundering of their lands. Much later, they asked each other if their family members in Heaven might have been watching over them.

The King brothers joined recruits from across Georgia to undergo a rigorous basic training program. Lordy and Neptune were the first to make the train trip to "Camp Georgia," set up in a pine grove near Richmond, Virginia. They were quickly organized into companies of one hundred men each, with ten companies in a regiment. The daily drills were severe and rigid military discipline was enacted. Enthusiasm ran high among the young soldiers, who accepted the unfamiliar military discipline as part of a new and exciting adventure.

The Georgia recruits came from every walk of life: planters, cotton factors, shopkeepers, lawyers, teachers and dirt farmers. None could have predicted the winding course of events that would take them from peaceful prewar Georgia to the bloody fields that lay ahead.

Their food consisted of beef, bacon, flour, cornmeal, rice,

hominy, coffee, sugar and salt and cabbage. Some soldiers got diarrhea or "green-apple quickstep" from eating poorly cooked food, and were sent back to the "Company Q" tent for some tea made from the bark of slippery elm, sweet gum or dogwood trees. If they had money, they could purchase fruits and vegetables and other meats from nearby villages. Neptune walked miles to buy Lordy's favorite ingredients, and then cooked him special suppers.

The new uniforms were worn with pride and honor. Their gray coats had ten horizontal black stripes along the front; each stripe with bright brass buttons at each end and in the center. Gilt embroidery trimmed their collars and cuffs, and more brass buttons with large epaulets gleamed on their shoulders. Their gray trousers had wide black stripes running down each outside leg seam. Gray forage caps topped off the ensemble.

The King women joined their neighbors and friends in knitting socks, sewing clothing, and bundling up packages to send to the soldiers. They sent them gloves, socks, underwear, shirts, sweaters, jackets and letters. Although the King boys left with trunks of clothing, silverware, fine linens and other treasures, the women knew that extra items from home would enable the soldiers to continue living like civilized gentlemen in camp.

Tootee sent her brothers weekly poems and items of interest she thought they would enjoy. One week Lordy and Neptune found this in their bundle.

"If in the early main of life,
You give yourself to God,
He'll stand by you mid earthly strife
And spare the chast'ning rod.
P.S. Roses are red and violets blue,
Sugar is sweet and so are you."

"It makes me miss home even more to read these words from my sisters," Lordy told Neptune, with a break in his voice.

The women also shared their concerns as they worked in small groups.

"I find it so hard not hearing from them yet. We don't know where they are for sure, and I'm worried," Georgia told her sisters and the others.

"You have a husband and four brothers fighting, you poor brave soul," said one of the older women in the circle with a sweet smile. "We will certainly pray for each of them."

"And our dear Neptune is also with Lordy, so please pray for him too," interjected Appy, now twenty-four years old.

"I give thanks that Mama didn't have to suffer through this war and our evacuation from Retreat. Maybe it's best she's resting with her Savior." Tootee had been thinking about that often and wanted to hear her sisters' opinions.

Georgia nodded. "Yes, Tootee, I think you're right. Mama would have been miserable without her sons, and not even hearing from them; especially with Papa so far away. I think it's a blessing that she was spared this anguish."

The soldiers marched through fields of wheat and clover. The lowland forests were filled with oaks, elms, hickories, maples, ash and conifers. Apple and peach orchards offered them their delicious red and yellow fruits, and sometimes they dug out peanuts as they walked through fields of "goobers." Their slaves followed behind them, always watchful and ready to attend to them. At least the weather favored them on this first march across Virginia and into the war.

Chapter Thirty-Four

August 16, 1862

Lordy was writing the last words in his long letter to his sisters. As he watched Neptune douse the campfire with water, he asked him if he wanted to add anything. Neptune turned around and told him that he wanted to send his love to each one.

"Oh, an' Mas' Lordy, tell Miss Georgia dat I be so happy she becum a nurse. An' den gib Colonel Duncan Smith my regard dat he now be a Brigadier General! We's so proud of dem, right?"

"That we are, Neptune. I do think my sister married a good man." Lordy settled back to read the letter one more time.

"*My beloved sisters,*

Your letters fill my heart with gladness. Both Neptune and I are so proud of you, Georgia, and your career as a volunteer nurse. Your stories of the primitive war hospitals with no anesthetics or narcotics were depressing and yet courageous. These experiences do help us grow in inexplicable ways.

Tootee, Flo and Appy, you also must keep the faith in your difficult conditions. Your refugee home and makeshift dwellings will one day provide fascinating stories for your children. We know the soil is not good and the crops were poor, but you have enough cotton to weave into clothes, corn to eat and feed the animals, and wild game in the woods. I know that our people will keep you safe and fed.

We travel from one place in Virginia to the next, and see the same sights. The children run about bare-footed, their clothes ragged and worn. Some of us are suffering similar conditions, but those of us who receive your loving care packages share them with our companions. The villages we pass through are miserable, and the people are unkempt. At least the weather is favorable for moving on.

We sing "Dixie," "Her Bright Smile Haunts Me Still," "Rock Me to Sleep, Mother," and "When I Saw Sweet Nellie Home" as we think about our families left behind. At night, we have prayer meetings after roll call. At the close of the services, our Chaplain of Legion invites soldiers to the Mercy Seat. And just last night a very moving occurrence happened.

From every part of the congregation came the soldiers, many with streaming eyes, giving the chaplain their hands and asking us to pray for them. So many came forward that the preacher decided to hold a baptism at the creek below our brigade. It was truly a beautiful sight to see General McLaws baptizing his men along with our chaplain.

Keep sending us the good sorghum syrup, the breads, pies and cakes, and the potatoes and peppers. Oh yes, and the onions are wonderful: so sweet and juicy! What would we do without you dear ones?

We have heard good news from soldiers in the 13th Regiment. Brother Mallery is now a Captain and Assistant Adjutant-General, and is in excellent health. But I'm certain that you heard this from him directly. I believe his West Point education has benefited him greatly. We have no news of brothers Floyd and Tip, but as Neptune says, 'De bad news come quick, so dey be fine.'

The diseases are still taking the lives of some of our men. Those who don't die are often disabled; they are sent to hospitals in Richmond. As you may remember, first it was the mea*sles, then pneumonia and typhoid fever. The doctors tell us much of it came from contaminated water or diseased milk. The men either died from the typhoid or got better—there is no treatment.*

Last week we waded across the Shenandoah River, but we were waist deep in water. We held our bundles over our heads, with the rifles tied on top. A ways after the river we passed the crest of the Blue Ridge Mountains and appreciated their beauty.

I don't want to write about the battles, because they are unpleasant details to relate. We are slowly defeating the Yankees, and soon the war will be over. Just know that I am well and unharmed. A little thinner than before, but in good health. When we are finally victorious, Neptune and I will return home, along with my brothers, and how joyously we will celebrate our reunion! Be in good spirits, and give my love and Neptune's to all those who love and pray for us.

Your devoted brother,
Henry Lord Page King"

Lordy and his fellow soldiers had recently been inspired by this message from General Robert E. Lee: "Duty is the most sublime word in our language. Do your duty in all things. You cannot do more. You should never wish to do less."

It was time to get some sleep. They would be moving forward again tomorrow morning. Neptune smiled as he thought about Ila. She would welcome news of them, and he knew in his heart that he would soon be with her and his precious children. This war would be over, and once again, they would be able to enjoy the moon shining over the marshlands.

Chapter Thirty-Five

November 20, 1862

Neptune looked over Lordy's supplies and decided he was pretty well fixed up for the winter. He found three shirts, three pairs of socks, a new pair of pants, a new coat and his uniform hat. Knowing that the trunk the King women sent them was lost in Petersburg, Neptune thought that they would make it through the cold times with the supplies they had between them.

It had recently turned cold and many of the men developed pleurisy and terrible coughs. The ones with pneumonia were sent away to the hospitals, and their troop doctors treated those who had bronchitis. The war was beginning to take its toll on their bodies and their dispositions. Many men were already dying of diseases, especially measles.

The ranks presented a distinctly ragged appearance. As they headed into winter, the soldiers voiced their doubts about seeing an end to the battles anytime soon. Although they were winning their battles, they agreed among themselves that the fighting had gone on too long. The men were wearing out.

Lordy remained unhurt through the battles of the Peninsula, Richmond, Sharpsburg and Harper's Ferry. Now they were preparing to join the corps near Fredericksburg, Virginia. The Yankee army was just beyond town, on the north bank of the Rappahannock River. Between them were the roofs and spires of Fredericksburg.Their division commander, Major General

Lafayette McLaws, called Lordy aside and asked him to be his "aide-de-camp." They spent several evenings together discussing battle strategies. Each night Lordy would return to Neptune and sit by his side, discussing war plans, sharing ideas, reading and writing letters, and revisiting old times on St. Simons Island.

Tonight, heads bowed before a dying campfire, Neptune and Lordy silently grieved the death of Georgia's husband, Brigadier General William Duncan Smith. The letter from Lordy's sisters told them that "Nurse Georgia" had ridden into action at her husband's side during the Battle of Manassas on August 30. Just over a month later, she was tragically widowed when he was killed in Charleston, South Carolina on October 4. Heartbroken, Georgia left the military and returned to Ware County, rejoining her sisters.

"Ay, Mas' Lordy, my heart bleeds fer Miss Georgia. Dis war be hurtin' our family too much." Neptune reached for the letter and pushed it in his pack. He stood up and walked toward the stream. Lordy watched him go.

Neptune sat beside the crystal stream, mingling his anguished tears with its sparkling waters. He sat for a long time, bathing his hot face and hands in the river. He was remembering and missing his mother, Missus Anna Matilda, Buttie, and the other King boys fighting the war. Tonight he saw the mission differently: he visualized the octopus arms of war, cruel and relentless. Nothing could comfort him tonight. He needed to figure out how to get through this thick, loud silence.

After an hour had passed, Lordy went to look for him and found him by their "abatis," a battlefield obstacle they had formed by cutting trees felled toward the enemy. Neptune was watching a wary young boy stepping carefully over the logs as he headed toward the campfire. This boy was one of 200,000 children who fought in the

Civil War, and like other young ones, he avoided the age requirement by signing on as a musician.

Lordy studied Neptune from a distance, respecting his pain. Neptune still sat by the water. After a long while Lordy returned alone to his tent, cold, weary and numb with sadness.

Later that night, Lordy suffered terrible nightmares. He saw himself and others in gray scrambling to their feet, forming their ranks and marching forward with steady tread toward the inferno that awaited them. He watched as desperate men were trying their hardest to blast the life out of each other. His dream took place in the summer, and he saw dense clouds of white, sulfurous powder smoke rolling across a countryside green with clover, golden with ripening wheat and checkered with patches of woodland.

Then the enemy gunners dropped shells into the Confederacy ranks. Men disintegrated under direct hits, or lost their legs to round shot that skipped across the ground like stones skipped across water. Shrapnel from other bursts knocked down three or four men at a time, but his gray line kept marching on. Smoke, dust, fence rails, rifles, caps and bodies sailed through the air, tossed about like rag dolls. Yet the soldiers scrambled to their feet again and again and formed up with the others to continue their advances toward the Union rifle pits.

"NO, OH GOD, NO!!!" screamed Lordy, sitting upright in the tent.

"Shh, Mas' Lordy, quiet. You be fine. You jes hab a bad dream," soothed Neptune, reaching over to rub his friend's back. "Hush up, boy, jes hush now."

Lordy sat alert, eyes bulging with fear.

"Oh Neptune, I saw my soldier friends running, shoulder to shoulder, toward the unseen enemy, yelling our fierce rebel yell, rising above the roar of battle. And the cannons were roaring, the shells bursting. And the wounded soldiers lay in the swamps crying, 'water, water.' It was the most horrific dream I've ever had. Oh, dear Lord," he whimpered.

"Mas' Lordy, it be jes a dream. It ain't happen' to us. We be winnin' de battles, remembah? Time to go back to sleep." Neptune prayed out loud to calm his nerves.

"No, Neptune. This is happening to us and to them, too. This is what happens in war. You know; you see it too." Lordy dropped his head, beaten down by his comprehension.

As he lay back on his mat and searched for relief in deep sleep, his mind flashed back to the conversation of his mother's dream, where he was holding his hand over his chest and bleeding everywhere. She had never shared it with him, but his brother, dear Buttie, told him about it. For the first time since becoming a soldier Lordy experienced true fear and anguish. He had nowhere to turn but to God.

Lord, you have my mother, my brothers and now my sister's husband with you. If I am to go next, make me worthy. Make me brave, strong, and capable as I continue to fight for my people. Let me die as a brave solder, and not a frightened coward. Please God, watch over my precious family, and most especially Neptune, who has given up everything to follow me. Amen.

When Neptune checked on him a moment later, he was fast asleep, his hands folded over his heart in prayer.

Chapter Thirty-six

December 13, 1862

Fog covered the valley of the Rappahannock River early morning of December 13. The Confederate regiments could hear Major General Burnside's Federal soldiers throwing pontoon bridges across the river at Fredericksburg, but could not see how many. General Lee countered with a brigade of sharpshooters firing from town houses, while the rest of the Confederate line waited. At 7:17 a.m., the sun rose red and fiery, promising a cloudless sky. The river was covered by a half inch of ice.

After arriving at Fredericksburg at the end of November, the Confederate soldiers spent their days resting and preparing for the next battle. They passed their free time in camp by rendering tallow into candles and cooking homemade soup. Neptune and some of the other slaves shared their recipes they had learned on the plantations. The weather was frosty but dry until the last few days of November. Then the clear skies gave way to rain. An extra shipment of clothes arrived from home just in time. The men had become tough; warm clothes, sound tents and a roaring log blaze seemed like all the comfort they could want.

On December 1, they awoke to torrents of white flakes spiraling through the bare limbs of the sycamores and spindly pine trees. The precise timing made the snowfall seem to be more than merely a sudden change of weather. It gave it the significance of an omen of what was to come.

In early December the Federal troops were camped out on the other side of the Rappahannock River. During the next few days, the Confederate army waited for them to cross the river. The Union gunboats at Port Royal exchanged artillery duels with the Confederate gunboats every day, but little damage was done to either side. The picket lines stationed on the riverbank talked back and forth to each other, as young men would do anywhere. They were ordered not to shoot at each other. Confederate General Lee's plan was to fall back and let the enemy cross over to them, so each day the soldiers on both sides expected the fighting would begin.

December 11 would see some of the bloodiest fighting of the war, on the hills of Marye's Heights west of Fredericksburg. The boom of the cannons brought the startled soldiers out of their tents. They scrambled to take up their rifles and moved into their assigned places. As they waited, they could hear the cannon thunder as the rival armies' artillery blasted away across the valley of the Rappahannock. The battle began when the Federal army tried to throw pontoon bridges across the river. The Federal army shelled the city all day, but the Confederate battery did not fire, hoping to give the impression that they didn't have much army at that site. At that point, the Yankees opted to set Fredericksburg on fire at 3 p.m. The following day, the cannon's roar continued to be heard everywhere.

When night fell cold and eerie on December 12 and the movement of troops and artillery continued, Neptune felt certain there would be a major battle the next day. As he cooked supper near the Confederate lines, he watched Lordy staring into the fire with a melancholy, far-away look in his eyes.

"Supper be ready, young Mausa."

Lordy stood and walked over to him. "Neptune, a big fight will happen tomorrow morning. A lot of good men will eat their last supper tonight." Lordy's eyes were haunted with despondency as he stood before Neptune.

"Ah, Mas' Lordy. You always bin so happy-hearted. Why you talk dis way tonite?" Neptune felt a ghostly chill wind drifting through his soul.

"Many good women could say 'husband' last Saturday morning when they arose. They will be widows when the sun sets tomorrow. Children that could say 'Father' yesterday will be orphans tomorrow. Ah, that God would intercede and give us peace once more." Lordy sat down and held out his bowl. "But His will be done, not ours."

Neptune sat beside him. Together they prayed; then they ate in silence.

Sometime later Neptune and Lordy walked up to Marye's Hill, high above the burning city. Looking down at the valley, they shook their heads in sadness.

"Let's go abed now, Mas' Lordy. Tomorrow be here too soon."

Chapter Thirty-seven

December 13, 1862

The air was alive with the hissing and humming of bullets. Shells from the cannons passed overhead and then exploded with ear-splitting booms, throwing clods of earth into the air. Neptune listened closely, trying to distinguish the yells and cheers. The Rebel yell was a discordant chorus of wails or yipping cries, high pitched and blood curdling. The Yankee cheers were organized, united cheers bellowed out in deep roars, sounding like "Hoo-Rah!" Neptune paid close attention, monitoring the battle from the hill.

Around 9 a.m. Major General Burnside sent his northern army forward against the Confederate positions, striking both the right and left sides but leaving the center position untouched. Midday, the Union forces scored a temporary success but were soon driven back by the men on lower ground, those positioned in front of the wooded ridge. Neptune knew that was the general area where Lordy was situated, and he suddenly felt as if he were lifted by currents he couldn't reverse. He knelt on the frigid ground and prayed for Lordy's safety.

Neptune could not know that after that strike Major General Lafayette McLaws requested a volunteer to carry dispatches to division commander Brigadier-General T.R.R. Cobb.

"I'll go," offered Captain Henry Lord Page King. "Send me."

Lordy fulfilled his mission, riding through the dangerous battlefield to deliver the orders. He pressed his charger Bell back through the whizzing bullets to return to his regiment. Halfway across the field, under strong enemy fire, he was struck down.

Neptune listened to the firing of cannons, followed by the musket rounds, but could no longer hear Rebel yells or Yankee cheers. Each time the wounded soldiers were brought back from the lines he searched fearfully for Lordy. Still the battle raged. Finally, the afternoon shadows fell and he watched the soldiers return to camp.

By nightfall, Neptune was worried. To ease his mind, he prepared supper.

Day ain't thru yet, he told himself. *I jes be patien' an' I sees Mas' Lordy walkin' ober here to me.* He stirred the fire again to keep their supper warm.

After dark, Neptune walked directly into the battlefield to look for Lordy. Searching up and down the rows of bodies, he ran into an officer he knew and asked him about Captain King.

"I haven't seen him since 2 p.m. or so, Neptune. He may be wounded if he's not back by now. Just look out for the Yankee pickets! "

Neptune headed toward the front line and crawled down the hill, avoiding the bullets flying from both sides. He walked back and forth between the wounded, the dying and the dead. He stopped and bent down over one young soldier, whose face was peaceful in death, as if he were quietly sleeping. Neptune's lip trembled when he noticed letters from his mother and sisters spread under his hand.

"Dead mans everwere but none look like Mas' Lordy," he mumbled to himself.

Another officer approached Neptune and asked him what he was doing. "Lookin' fer my youn' mausa, Mas' Lord King."

"That's him over there, lying face down," responded the officer, weariness and pity etched across his face as he softly touched Neptune's arm and pointed.

Neptune had passed this blood-covered officer earlier, refusing to believe it was Lordy. He hesitated, and suddenly remembered how he and Anna Matilda used to run their hands through his thick, curly, raven hair. Stooping over, Neptune lightly touched the blood encrusted black hair. The first rush of disbelief brought him to his knees.

Neptune slowly turned him over. The tears rolling down his cheeks spilled unchecked onto his clothing. His hands had no feeling whatsoever. Someone had stolen one of Lordy's boots, leaving the other because it was too bloody. As if from a distance, Neptune heard himself wailing, "*NO, NO, NO, NOOO!*"

He sat for a while, weeping for Lordy. Then he brushed away the tears and spoke to him. "Mas' Lordy, dis is ole Neptune. Supper ready. I bin waitin' on you. Is you hurt bad?"

Lordy didn't answer. Neptune picked up his body and held him close to his heart. He wanted to stay right on that spot until Lordy woke up and responded. He didn't want to do anything else. He would have to wait there until he could move.

In the distance, the shells burst and the bullets rattled.

"Don't pay no mind to dat, Mas' Lordy. Dey cain't hurt you an' ole Neptune don't care bout hisself. You come wif me an' we go home."

The general who had spoken to him earlier rode up. He dismounted and sat down next to Neptune.

"Neptune, Captain King was a brave and gallant officer. He died serving his commander, and he'll be remembered and honored. Please accept my simple words of sympathy."

Neptune lowered his head in agreement. Then he struggled to his feet.

Together they lifted Lordy and draped him over Neptune's

shoulder, his waist bending over Neptune's shoulder bone and his arms dangling forward.

"Suh, I be takin' my mausa to wash clean now. Den I take him home fer a Christian buryin'."

The officer nodded. He offered to carry Lordy on his own horse to the campsite. Neptune thanked him, but explained that he needed to carry his master himself.

I feel de breath rippin' frum my lungs, an' my stomick turns ober an' ober. I carry my Mas' Lordy to his camp, an' I wash him up clean. My dear God, I sees 17 holes in his precious body, but he don't hurt no mo'. I wanna sit in de road an' stay fer de rest of my life. But I gotta get my mausa home; we gotta go to his family.

A warm south wind swept away some of the chill of the December night. Up the Rappahannock, to the left of the campsite, the sky began to glow. Some of the soldiers guessed it was their cavalry burning supplies. The sky grew dark again, and the lights returned in a different color, so bright that it lit up the faces of the soldiers. Then it changed colors again. This was the first time the southern soldiers had experienced the Northern Lights, and some felt sure they were banners promising ultimate victory.

But Neptune looked up to the heavens and smiled wistfully.

"I hears you, Mas' Lordy. You be tellin' me you safe wif yo' Maker."

The next morning several officers from Lordy's regiment brought Neptune the horse Lordy had ridden to carry the dispatch. They helped him place Captain King's body in a simple pine coffin. As they closed it up, Neptune noticed a butterfly resting like a sunbeam on the lid. A moment later it lifted its wings and flew away. He reflected on how its beauty belonged to him for just a brief moment. Gratefully, he touched his lips to the coffin and felt Lordy's glory.

Then he reached over and stroked Bell's neck.

"Ready, girl?" he asked her, looking back at the pine box. "We gunna take him home now."

"If you see my mother
Oh yes,
Won't you tell her for me?
Oh yes,
I'm a riding my horse in the battle-field
I want a see my Jesus in the mornin'.
Ride on King
Ride on Conquerin' King
I wanna see my Jesus in de mornin'."

Epilogue

Neptune Small struggled through the bitter winter along rugged trails, rivers, marshes and forests to return Captain Henry Lord King's body to his family. When he reached Richmond, Virginia he purchased the best coffin he could find and then continued on to Savannah, Georgia, walking over five hundred miles from beginning to end. In a tearful and loving reunion, Lordy's brothers and sisters joined Neptune in Savannah. They buried their brother in a temporary grave at Laurel Grove Cemetery on Christmas Day of 1862. At the end of the war, when he could be safely returned to St. Simons Island, Henry Lord Page King was laid to rest in the family plot at Christ Church.

Thomas Butler King sent word to Neptune that he had done enough; he did not need to return to the front. Yet Neptune insisted on going back to accompany the youngest King son, Richard Cuyler, "Tip." He would not be dissuaded, and he stayed with Tip until the Confederate forces surrendered in 1865. The three remaining King brothers fought gallantly in more than one hundred engagements, yet were never wounded. All of them returned to St. Simons Island after the war.

Lordy's Commander, Brigadier General T.R.R. Cobb, was mortally wounded in the heat of the battle of December 13, 1862, the same day that Captain Henry Lord Page King was killed.

Thomas Butler King's health continued to fail during the time he was representing the Confederacy abroad. Somehow he was able to escape the blockage forces and return to spend his final days with his daughters in Ware County, Georgia. He eventually died of pneumonia on May 10, 1864, surrounded by his daughters, grandchildren and son-in-law, before all hope of victory had passed. He was laid to rest beside his wife Anna Matilda in Christ Church Cemetery.

Mallery Page King, "Malley," married his childhood friend Eugenia Grant while on leave from war in late 1862. Georgia, Appy and Florence King all married soon after the war's end, and went to live in Savannah, Georgia. Tootee, William and their children eventually made their home in Marietta, Georgia. Floyd, "Fuddy," never married. He followed in his father's footsteps and went into politics, serving as a U.S. Congressman for his adopted state of Louisiana. Tip, the youngest son, finally married in his late forties.

When the King family returned to their St. Simons Island and their lovingly remembered home, they found total desolation and destruction. Anna Matilda's once famous gardens were reduced to choking jungles; the happy and beautiful home was now a devastated and plundered shell of antebellum days. The plantations lay stripped of everything of value; even the citrus groves and orchards were trampled and destroyed. Christ Church Frederica was in ruins, with the surrounding graves robbed and desecrated. All was changed, except the pounding surf, the exquisite lands and the love and loyalty of a handful of their former slaves.

Malley returned to live on Retreat Plantation and tried to maintain the cotton fields there and the rice fields on the mainland. Eventually, he had to forfeit the 2,000 acres the King children had inherited from the estate of their mother.

The remaining Retreat property was held by Virginia and put in trust for Malley's three daughters. These included land on St.

Simons Sound; land stretching from Frederica River on the west to St. Simons Lighthouse on the east, and "King City." King City is now the residential and commercial area known as the "Village," where the streets are named after the King children. At the end of Mallery Street sits Neptune Park, located on the land given to Neptune Small by the King family after the war.

When the war was over, Neptune was awarded his freedom. In addition, as a reward for his service to Lordy, the Kings gifted him a piece of land on the southern edge of the Retreat property, where he built his house. He and Ila had a total of five children: Leanora, Louturia, Clementine, Cornielia and Clarence. "Daddy" Neptune was honored and respected by all who knew him. Although now a free man, he chose to remain with the King family, helping them rebuild, doing maintenance chores and tending the cemetery where his beloved Lordy was buried.

Captain Henry Lord Page King's body was finally brought back to St. Simons Island and reburied in Christ Church Cemetery, where Neptune cared for it as devotedly as he had cared for Lordy in life. He continued to clean leaves and rubbish from the cemetery and keep the grass cropped until he was old, stooped and white-haired.

Since there were no surnames in use among the Negro slaves before the war, Neptune was able to choose his own when he became a free man. With his keen sense of humor and fun, he chose the last name of "Small," because of his own stature.

Neptune Small passed away on August 10, 1907, at the age of seventy-five. After his death, a portion of his property was sold to the city of St. Simons and turned into a park that bears his name. He is buried next to a lily-covered pond in a small shady cemetery reserved for Retreat Plantation slaves and their descendants. His bronze tablet tombstone tells the story of his devotion to the King family, and portrays the highest esteem and affection they held for him.

"Neptune belonged to Mr. and Mrs. Thomas Butler King of Retreat Plantation. When their son Captain Henry Lord Page King enlisted in the Confederate Army, Neptune accompanied him to war as his body-servant. Captain King was killed at the battle of Fredericksburg, VA on December 13, 1862. When night fell Neptune went out on the battlefield, found the body of his master and brought it home to rest in the family burying ground at Christ Church Frederica, St. Simons Island."

Neptune Small (Courtesy of Coastal Georgia Historical Society)

Neptune's Tombstone, Retreat Plantation Slave Cemetery (Courtesy of Coastal Georgia Historical Society)

Acknowledgments

My introduction to Neptune Small's story came about the first week we moved to St. Simons Island. My husband and I took the St. Simons Trolley Island Tour and learned about the history of Neptune Park. The story was intriguing and deeply touched us. Over the next two years, as friends and family came to visit and took the tour with me, I began to appreciate the extent of Neptune's love and loyalty to the family who owned him. Every time Bunny and Jenny related the story, I wondered why I could not find a book about Neptune's life. Finally, I decided that I would write his story. Thank you, Jenny Strauss and Bunny Marshall, for bringing Neptune into my life!

There were several books, mostly local, that touched briefly on Neptune's story. As I delved deeper into my research of the Thomas Butler King family and Retreat Plantation, I discovered an exciting new book, *Anna, The Letters of a St. Simons Island Plantation Mistress, 1817–1859*, by Melanie Pavich-Lindsay. Based on actual letters written by Thomas Butler King's wife Anna Matilda, a complete portrait of their antebellum Southern plantation life was painted for me. Neptune Small's world began opening up and I was able to re-create his life; first in my heart and finally, on paper. Melanie, thank you so much for your masterpiece, which became my primary source for *Neptune's Honor*. And thank you for assisting me greatly by reading and commenting on my manuscript.

Because Neptune's story took place during the Civil War era, it was impossible to hear his stories first-hand. However, stories were passed down through the family, and I was very fortunate to have opportunities to speak to some of his descendants. Miss Creola Barnes Belton, Neptune's great-grandchild, very graciously agreed to speak with me. Her niece, Miss Diane Palmer Haywood and her daughter, Angie Palmer, brought me Neptune's family tree and articles family members had written about him. They also agreed to read my manuscript and gave me feedback, allowing me to present Neptune's story more accurately. I thank each one of them from the bottom of my heart!

Also, a heartfelt thanks to my friend Gwen Davis for introducing me to these wonderful ladies! You got me started on this fantastic journey!

Buddy Sullivan, well-known Coastal Georgia historian, renowned author, educator, Sapelo Island National Estuarine Research Reserve manager, and friend: you are such an inspiration to me! You wear so many hats and do it all so well. Thank you for reading my manuscript, giving me pointers, and setting such an outstanding example for writers! Thank you for your endorsement. My curiosity about the history of this amazing part of the world originated at your Coastal Georgia presentations, which are a "must do" for everyone interested in this area.

I owe so much to our local bookstores! Everyone who works in them has done a great service to me in so many ways. Brian Trainor, thank you for providing me with a centrally located stand for all my books in your bookstore. And you helped me find Mr. Earnest Butts, our cover artist!

Nancy Thomason, you constantly keep me updated with local political activities and coach me on book marketing, while hand-selling my books as I sit beside you! Wendy Beeker, I am so grateful to you for book signings each time I write a book! Thank you Pat Weaver for the chance to exhibit in your art shows and for carrying my books in your gallery! Mary Jane, Bill, Wendy, Lynne, Mary Ashley, Georgia, Heather, Tommye, Beverly and all the rest of you have shown me how beautifully this literary community supports its authors! Thank you, thank you!

Our local libraries provided me with hours of enjoyable research. The first one I visited was the Arthur J. Moore/United Methodist Museum, offering book after book about this island and its plantation families. The Coastal Georgia Historical Society graciously shared their files and photographs with me. I particularly want to thank Pat Morris and Mia Knight-Nichols for searching through stacks of catalogs to locate what I needed. I also spent many afternoons of research in both the St. Simons Public Library and the Brunswick-Glynn County Regional Library and I thank them for their resources! My good friend Cary Knapp, columnist and librarian at the Brunswick-Glynn County Regional Library, has always been there for me whenever I asked her.

To my friend Jeff Hoffman: thanks for taking me to Neptune's grave and shooting photos for the back cover. Harry Aiken, busy man that you are, thanks for taking the time to read and give me feedback on the manuscript. This was very important to me because Harry is a direct descendant of Mallery King.

Victor Howard, local publisher, author, and friend brought me a remarkable out-of-print research book on the Confederate Rebels. Another friend, Suzie Koller, offered me copies of her relatives' Confederate letters, written before and during the days of the Battle of Fredericksburg. Thank you both so much!

My dear friend Trip Giudici, local author and descendant of John Couper, helped me organize my outline for this story, and then sat with me to edit and re-write many chapters during revision stages. I would never have finished this book by deadline without his expertise! Thank you Trip, for giving me so much time, help and ideas!

Trip introduced me to William Barnes Jr., Neptune's great-great grandson from Texas. William is the family historian and was able to send me birth dates of Neptune's family as well as providing excellent feedback on the manuscript. He spent hours working with me on revisions, even suggesting some of the dialogue! Thank you, William, for your support and your remarks!

I remain in deep gratitude to my cover artist, Earnest Butts Jr. Having admired his work in local galleries, I phoned him to ask if he were interested in working with me on this book. I explained the significance of having an African-American artist paint Neptune's cover, and then gave him some general ideas of what I was looking for. Two weeks later he showed me his remarkable painting: an exquisite portrayal of Neptune and Lordy's bond.

This is the fifth book that my faithful publishing team has brought to life. Thank you again, Patty Osborne, for taking my manuscript, ideas, and cover art and turning them into beautiful books. Thank you, Ray Hignell, for locating the best printing teams possible, meeting our deadlines, and patiently answering my questions. Pamela Pollack started with me on my first children's book and has remained faithful as my "book doctor," offering me creative suggestions that always improved my focus and writing. Sharon Castlen, my publicist and friend, thank you for doing an excellent job of guiding me through the book marketing procedures. You've all taught me to make work fun!

The day I finished writing the revisions, I returned to the Christ Church Cemetery to pay tribute to all my historical friends. As I stood in front of Lordy's tombstone, I was approached by an enchanting southern couple, Betty and James

Lamberth, offering to tell me about the King family. I smiled, and explained that I knew them well, and that opened up a new friendship. I thank them so much for making the final writing day particularly special.

I would like to thank my awesome mother, Phyllis Bauer, for introducing me to Eugenia Price, who has made history come to life through all of her St. Simons characters. My mother read her novels long before I moved to this enchanted island, and she gave me her books to read. What a blessing! Ms. Eugenia Price is such an extraordinary example of what an historical novelist should be! Thank you, Mom, for this thoughtful gift!

I reserve the warmest, most loving thank you for my beloved husband, Michael. This dear, caring, understanding and patient man has worked with me 200% on the researching, editing, marketing and business aspect of all our books. I would never have been able to embark on this journey without you. I love you and truly appreciate your generosity in giving me this opportunity to do what I love!

There were many instances where I couldn't find the words to write, but my Lord God could. I am only an instrument through which God can work. I am so indebted to Him and His grace. Thank you, dear Lord, for promising that our prayers would be heard.

"*For everyone who asks receives; he who seeks finds; and to him who knocks, the door will be opened.*" (Luke 11:10)

RESOURCES

PRINTED WORD

Primary Source

Pavich-Lindsay, Melanie, editor. *Anna, The Letters of a St. Simons Island Plantation Mistress, 1817-1859*. Athens, GA. The University of Georgia Press. 2002.

Secondary Sources

Cate, Margaret Davis. *Early Days of Coastal Georgia.* Brunswick, GA. Galley Press. 1955.

Cate, Margaret Davis. *Our Todays and Yesterdays.* Brunswick, GA. Glover Press Inc. 1972.

Dart, J.E. "Neptune's Story" from *Old Mill Days: St. Simons Mills, Georgia*, Circa *1874-1908* Newspaper.

Gay, Mary A.H. *Life in Dixie During the War.* Macon, GA. Mercer University Press. Edited by **J.H. Segars.** First published in 1892.

Howard, Robert West, Editor. *This Is The South.* Tuscon, Arizona. Happy Jack Enterprises. 1959.

Huie, Mildred Nix and **Wilcox, Mildred H.** *King's Retreat Plantation, St. Simons Island, Georgia; Today and Yesterday.* St. Simons Island, GA. Bessie Lewis. 1980.

Hull, Barbara. *St. Simons Enchanted Island.* Savannah, GA. Cherokee Publishing Co. 1980.

Johnson, Amanda. *Georgia As A Colony and State.* Savannah, GA. Cherokee Publishing Co. 1970.

King, Spencer B. Jr. *Georgia Voices.* Athens, GA. University of Georgia Press. 1966.

Lane, Mills. *Dear Mother, Don't Grieve About Me. If I Get*

Killed, I'll Only Be Dead: Letters from Georgia Soldiers in the Civil War. Savannah, GA. The Beehive Press. 1977.

Lane, Mills. *The People of Georgia.* Savannah, GA. The Beehive Press. 1975.

Lovell, Caroline Couper. *The Golden Isles of Georgia.* New York. Little, Brown and Co. 1933.

Mayre, Florence. *The Story of The Page-King Family of Retreat Plantation, St. Simons Island, and of the Golden Isles of Georgia.* Darien, GA. Darien Printing and Graphics. Edited by **Edwin R. MacKethan** III. 2000.

Murray, Alton. *South Georgia Rebels.* St. Mary's, GA. Alton J. Murray. 1976.

Parrish, Lydia. *Slave Songs of the Sea Islands.* Athens, GA. The University of Georgia Press. 1942.

Perkerson, Medora Field. *White Columns in Georgia.* New York. Bonanza Books. 1956.

Pond, Cornelia Jones. *Life On A Liberty County Plantation.* Athens, GA. The University of Georgia Press. 1974. Edited by **Josephine Bacon Marlin.**

Price, Eugenia. *Where Shadows Go.* New York. Doubleday. 1993.

Price, Eugenia. *Beauty from Ashes.* New York. Doubldday. 1995.

Rivers, Nancy Fowler. *A New Life for Toby.* Franklin, TN. Hillsboro Press. 1997.

Rosengarten, Theodore. *Tomba – Portrait of a Cotton Planter.* New York. William Morrow and Co., Inc. 1986.

Stroyer, Jacob. *My Life in the South.* Salem MA. Salem Observer Book and Job Print. 1885.

Sullivan, Buddy (in association with **The Georgia Historical Society**). *Georgia, A State History.* Charleston, S.C. Arcadia Publishing. 2003.

Wilkenson, Warren and **Woodsworth, Steven.** *A Scythe of Fire.* New York. Harper Collins Publishers Inc. 2002.

ARTICLES

Jones, Sandy. *The Story of Neptune Small.* Sea Island, GA. Sea Is. Festival. 1992.

Palmer, Diondre Solomon. *The Story of Neptune Small.* A tribute from a descendant. 1999.

CONFEDERATE LETTERS

My friend **Susie Few Koller** presented me with copies of five letters written by two of her ancestors, Confederate Soldiers Napoleon B. Durham and Edgar Richardson. These letters were written between December 11, 1862 and August 7, 1863. Judging by the content of the letters, it is quite possible that these two soldiers fought in Captain Henry Lord Page King's regiment. The valuable letters were left in a cowhide-covered trunk to her great-great grandfather, Mr. Sam Few.

INTERVIEWS

Mr. Harry Aiken, great-great grandson of Mallery Butler King.

Miss Creola Barnes Belton, great-granddaughter of Neptune Small.

Mr. William Barnes, great-great-grandson of Neptune Small.

Mr. Carey "Trip" Giudici, great-great grandson of John (Jock) Couper.

Miss Diane Palmer Haywood, great-great niece of Neptune Small.

Miss Angie Palmer, daughter of Miss Diane Palmer Haywood.

Ms. Melanie Pavich-Lindsay, editor of *Anna, The Letters of a St. Simons Island Plantation Mistress, 1817-1859.*

Mr. Buddy Sullivan, renowned Coastal Georgia historian, author, educator.

ABOUT THE ARTIST

Earnest Butts Jr. was born near Albany, Georgia but was raised as a young child on St. Simons Island, Georgia. He is one of five children of Earnest and Lillie P. Butts, who reside in the Brunswick, Georgia area.

Earnest attended school in Brunswick, Georgia and graduated from Glynn Academy High. Even from an early age, he was fascinated with art. While in high school, he studied art under Mary Griffith, Laura Edenfield and Steve Collins. After high school, he began to paint under the tutelage of the late Bill Hendrix at the Coastal Center for the Arts on St. Simons Island. He also studied art at the Coastal Georgia Community College in Brunswick.

Earnest likes to paint elongated paintings in acrylic. His work ranges from bold color to simple pencil drawings. His subject matter spans from fantasy compositions to animal and human topics.

Earnest resides in Brunswick, Georgia and continues to enjoy sharing with and passing on the gift of his paintings to those who appreciate them.

ABOUT THE AUTHOR

Pamela Bauer Mueller was raised in Oregon and graduated from Lewis and Clark College in Portland, Oregon. She worked as a flight attendant for Pan American Airlines before moving to Mexico City, where she lived for eighteen years. Pamela is bicultural as well as bilingual. She has worked as a commercial model, an actress, and an English and Spanish language instructor during her years in Mexico.

After returning to the United States, Pamela worked for twelve years as a U.S. Customs inspector. She served six years in San Diego, California and then was selected to work a foreign assignment in Vancouver, British Columbia, Canada. Pamela took an early retirement from U.S. Customs to follow her husband Michael, who received an instructor position at the Federal Law Enforcement Training Center in Brunswick, Georgia.

Pamela and Michael reside on Jekyll Island, Georgia with their cats, Jasper and Sukey Spice. Pamela wrote *Eight Paws to Georgia*, *Hello, Goodbye, I Love You*, *Neptune's Honor*, *An Angry Drum Echoed* and *Aloha Crossing* after moving to Georgia. *Neptune's Honor* is her first historical fiction, and is based on actual residents of St. Simons Island during the pre-Civil War antebellum era.